Allie Finkle's RULES for GIRLS

Book Five:
Glitter Girls and the Great Fake Out

Books by MEG CABOT

Allie Finkle's Rules for Girls #1: *Moving Day*
Allie Finkle's Rules for Girls #2: *The New Girl*
Allie Finkle's Rules for Girls #3: *Best Friends and Drama Queens*
Allie Finkle's Rules for Girls #4: *Stage Fright*
Allie Finkle's Rules for Girls #5: *Glitter Girls and the Great Fake Out*

FOR TEENS

Airhead
Being Nikki
All-American Girl
Ready or Not
Teen Idol
How to Be Popular
Pants on Fire
Jinx
Nicola and the Viscount
Victoria and the Rogue

The Princess Diaries series
The Mediator series
1-800-Where-R-You series
Avalon High series

**For a complete list of Meg Cabot's books,
please visit www.megcabot.com**

Allie Finkle's RULES for GIRLS

Book Five:

Glitter Girls and the Great Fake Out

Books by MEG CABOT

Allie Finkle's Rules for Girls #1: *Moving Day*
Allie Finkle's Rules for Girls #2: *The New Girl*
Allie Finkle's Rules for Girls #3: *Best Friends and Drama Queens*
Allie Finkle's Rules for Girls #4: *Stage Fright*
Allie Finkle's Rules for Girls #5: *Glitter Girls and the Great Fake Out*

FOR TEENS

Airhead
Being Nikki
All-American Girl
Ready or Not
Teen Idol
How to Be Popular
Pants on Fire
Jinx
Nicola and the Viscount
Victoria and the Rogue

The Princess Diaries series
The Mediator series
1-800-Where-R-You series
Avalon High series

**For a complete list of Meg Cabot's books,
please visit www.megcabot.com**

MEG CABOT

Allie Finkle's RULES for GIRLS

Book Five:

Glitter Girls and the Great Fake Out

SCHOLASTIC PRESS · NEW YORK
An Imprint of Scholastic Inc.

Library of Congress Cataloging-in-Publication Data

Cabot, Meg.
   Glitter girls and the great fake out / Meg Cabot. — 1st ed.
    p. cm. — (Allie Finkle's rules for girls ; bk. 5)
   Summary: While trying to spare Erica's feelings so she could go to
Brittany's birthday party, Allie disobeys one of her own rules and lies.
   ISBN 978-0-545-04047-1
   [1. Honesty — Fiction. 2. Birthdays — Fiction. 3. Parties — Fiction.
4. Rules (Philosophy) — Fiction. 5. Behavior — Fiction. 6. Friendship —
Fiction.] I. Title.
   PZ7.C11165Gl 2010
   [Fic] — dc22

                       2009032125

10 9 8 7 6 5 4 3 2 1

Printed in the U.S.A. 23
First edition, March 2010

The display type was set in Chaloops and Yellabelly.
The text type was set in Centaur MT Regular.
Book design by Elizabeth B. Parisi

For glitter girls everywhere

Many thanks to Beth Ader, Jennifer Brown, Laura Langlie, Becky Lee at Blue Willow Bookshop, Abigail McAden, and especially Benjamin Egnatz

RULE #1

It's Important to Try Not to Hurt Someone's Feelings If You Can Help It

"Is that the one you're going to wear?" I stared at the red-spangled bodysuit Erica's older sister, Missy, had on.

I could hardly believe how beautiful she looked in it. Usually when I saw Missy, she had on sweatpants.

Sweatpants and a really mean expression as she was slamming her bedroom door in my face.

It wouldn't be an exaggeration to say that Missy hated my guts.

But then Missy hated the guts of all of Erica's friends, so I didn't take it personally. Missy hated Erica, too, even

I

though Erica refused to believe it and was always trying to do nice things for her big sister.

Like right now, for instance, Erica had enlisted our help in getting Missy to decide which of her six fanciest baton-twirling costumes she should wear for the seventh annual Little Miss Majorette Baton Twirling Twirltacular, middle school division.

"I think you should wear the blue one," Rosemary said.

"The blue one doesn't have as much glitter," Sophie said, from Missy's bed, where we were sitting all in a row while Missy was putting on her fashion show for us. "Only sparkly fringe."

This was the first time we'd ever been invited into Missy's bedroom after school, so it was truly a huge occasion, and we were trying very hard not to break the rules Missy had explained to us before she'd allowed us to come in.

The rules were: 1. Do not touch anything, 2. No talking unless Missy says you can talk, and 3. Leave the minute Missy says so.

Break the rules, and Missy will break *you.*

"I know," Rosemary said. "That's why I like the blue one."

"The red one is definitely sparklier," Caroline said. "Although 'sparklier' isn't a word."

Caroline would know. She was our class spelling champion, even though she lost the district spelling bee.

"I just can't decide," Missy said with a sigh as she fluffed out her blond hair and stared at herself in her full-length mirror. "I do look amazing in all of them, don't I?"

"Yes," we all said in unison.

Always agree with everything Missy says if you want her to stay in a good mood. This was another rule.

Being friends with Erica was very good training in how to deal with teenagers. Also how not to act when I become one. Because Missy was really moody. Also rude. At least most of the time. She was being nice to us today, though, because she wanted our help deciding what to wear to the Little Miss Majorette Baton Twirling Twirltacular.

I won't lie: I wanted to go to the Little Miss Majorette Baton Twirling Twirltacular more than I had ever wanted to go anywhere in my whole entire life. At least, ever since I'd heard about it (a half hour earlier).

Because Missy and Erica and Mrs. Harrington (who had hand-sewn all of Missy's costumes for her) had told us about it while we were eating after-school snacks of fruit and graham crackers in the kitchen of their house.

And it sounded like the most exciting thing in the world.

First of all, twirlers (that's what the people who spin and toss batons are called. Twirlers. Also majorettes, but "twirler" is more correct because a twirler can be a boy *or* a girl, whereas majorettes are only girls) come from all over the state — possibly even from *outside* the state — to participate in the Twirltacular, which lasts a whole weekend.

At the Twirltacular, there are events in dance, strut, teams, showtwirls, solos, multiple batons, flags, hoops, and duets/pairs.

I didn't exactly know what any of that means, but I totally wanted to see it. In fact, the more I heard about it from Erica and Mrs. Harrington and Missy, the more I thought I would *die* if I didn't get to see it.

And I was really lucky because the Little Miss Majorette Baton Twirling Twirltacular was happening right here in my *very own town*.

Missy said if we didn't act like ingrates, which means ungrateful people, we could come watch her compete.

So there was a chance I might actually get to see her perform at the Little Miss Majorette Baton Twirling Twirltacular, middle school division. My friends Sophie, Caroline, and I decided that we were going to go with Erica on Saturday, in order to show our support for her sister.

Our friend Rosemary wasn't sure if she wanted to go or not. She thought twirling sounded very boring, despite all the sparkles.

But of course she hadn't said so in front of Missy, because that would hurt Missy's feelings.

It's important to try not to hurt someone's feelings if you can help it. That's a rule.

It's especially important to try not to hurt Missy's feelings, because she is much bigger than we are and when you do something she doesn't like, she'll tackle you and sit on you and then spit in your face. She's done this to me before and it was really gross.

Missy's parents, Mr. and Mrs. Harrington, were going to the Little Miss Majorette Baton Twirling Twirltacular, of course. So was John, Erica and Missy's older brother. At first, Erica said, John didn't want to go. Like Rosemary, John thought twirling was boring.

But then after John saw Missy's leotards, he asked if there'd be any girls his own age at the event, and Mrs. Harrington said yes there would be, since the competition went from sixth to eighth grade, which was John's grade.

So then John said maybe he might like to go after all.

The grand prizewinners in each event at the Twirltacular, Missy said, get a trophy that's as big as me. At the top of the trophy is a statue of a little gold lady twirling a baton (if you're a boy twirler, you get a little gold man, Missy said, although she doubted there would be any boy twirlers at the Little Miss Majorette Baton Twirling Twirltacular).

I wanted Missy to get one of these trophies. I wanted her to get one very, very much.

And I wanted to be there when she got it. I wanted to be there to help support her, to cheer her on, and to eat the popcorn that Erica said they always sell in little paper bags at the middle school whenever they have these events. *Good News!*, the local cable television news show where my mother does movie reviews, might even be there to report on the event. They came last year, Erica said.

"I think you should wear the lime green one with the rhinestone fringe," Erica said to Missy. "And the rainbow one with the purple glitter."

"That's my favorite," Sophie said, sounding as if her heart was aching because she wanted to have a rainbow-colored leotard covered in sequins, with purple glittery fringe dangling down from the leg holes.

I knew how Sophie felt, because I felt exactly the same way. I wanted one of those baton-twirling costumes, but I don't know how to twirl a baton (although I've practiced a bit in the front yard with one of Missy's old batons that she doesn't use anymore. The problem was, the baton fell down from the tree, where I accidentally threw it, and hit me in the head. After that I decided to just stick with ballet, which I do on Saturdays and also Wednesdays after school, and softball on the Girls Club team in the summertime).

"Yeah," Missy said, thoughtfully baring her teeth and examining her electric blue braces in the mirror. "I think you guys are right. I'll wear the rainbow one for my dance routine and the green one for my solo."

Then Missy signaled to Erica to turn on her CD player. And so Erica did, and Missy's song for her twirling solo came on, and Missy started practicing it in the mirror. The song was called "I'm Gonna Knock You Out," and it was playing very, very loud.

So loud that I'm sure Sophie thought Missy couldn't hear her when she leaned over to whisper to us, "You guys, we *have* to go see Missy perform on Saturday."

Erica looked over at her sister, whose back was to us as she performed in front of the mirror. "Shhh," she said, in a panicky way. "She'll hear you! She said no talking, remember?"

"I know," Sophie said. "But I just think it's really important we all go on Saturday. To support Missy. I think she
has problems with her self-esteem. That's why she's so
bossy. Allie, are you sure you can go? Don't you have ballet
on Saturday?"

I had forgotten I had ballet with Madame Linda on
Saturday. My parents pay in advance for my lessons, too.

"That's okay," I said. "I'm sure I can skip my lesson this
one time."

This was a lie. But it was just a very small lie. I was sure
it didn't matter. Very much.

"That's good," Sophie said. "What about you, Caroline?"

"Oh, I can go," Caroline said. "I have my Mandarin lesson, but it's just with my dad. I can do it anytime."

"You guys," Rosemary said, when she saw we were all
looking at her. "I don't want to go. And I don't think anything is wrong with Missy's self-esteem. She's just a brat.
And baton twirling is boring."

"It's not boring," Sophie said, looking offended. "It's a
very beautiful form of self-expression."

"Missy is kind of bossy," Erica admitted. "But she doesn't have very many friends. She could really use our support."

"Teenage hormones," Caroline said knowingly. "I've read about this. You're right. We have to support her."

It was kind of funny that right at that moment Missy turned around and, looking enraged, yelled, "I said no talking!"

We all knew what was coming next. We jumped from Missy's bed and ran for her bedroom door before she could leap on any of us, knock us down, and sit on us.

Thinking about what might happen after that was too terrible even to contemplate.

Fortunately, we all made it out into the safety of the hallway, where Mrs. Harrington happened to be walking by with another of Missy's twirling costumes, which she had been hemming down in her studio, where she also makes fine collectibles, such as dollhouse furniture and miniature felt toadstools with tiny lady dwarves sitting on them, to sell in her shop downtown.

"Good heavens," Mrs. Harrington said when we all came tumbling out of Missy's room at the same time. "What's going on?"

"Nothing," we chimed together, coming to a halt right in front of her.

When Missy saw her mom, she pointed an accusing finger at us and said, "That's not true! I was performing my dance routine for Saturday, and they started talking! It broke my concentration."

"Well, honey," Mrs. Harrington said, looking completely unruffled, though Missy looked as if she was about to cry. Really! She had tears in her eyes, and everything (except that they were fake tears, if you ask me). "I'm sure the girls didn't mean any disrespect. And you're going to have to get used to people talking during your performances, Missy. There are going to be all sorts of distractions this weekend. People talking, other girls and boys doing their routines at the same time yours is going on." Also, people eating popcorn. "You're really going to need to learn how to focus and block them all out, sweetie."

Our eyes wide, we glanced over at Missy to see how she'd handle this information. She narrowed her eyes at her mother, then fixed each of us with a glare that could have melted snow.

Then she turned around and stormed back into her room, slamming the door behind her.

"Excuse me," Mrs. Harrington called after her. "But we do not slam doors around here, young lady!"

This was a rule.

"Sorry," Missy called, from inside her room.

But if you ask me, she didn't sound sorry at all.

"I'm sorry about that, Mrs. Harrington," Rosemary said. Rosemary was very good about apologizing to adults. "We didn't mean to make Missy upset. And those glittery costumes you made for her are awfully nice."

"Why, thank you, Rosemary!" Mrs. Harrington beamed. "I'm very flattered you like them. If you'd like to take up twirling, I'd be happy to make you one, as well. Twirling's such a lovely sport. I think any one of you girls would be very good at it."

The idea of Rosemary, whose favorite sport was

football — especially the part where you get to tackle people and hold them to the ground — daintily prancing around a dance floor while spinning a baton was so hilarious that for a minute it was all I could do to keep myself from bursting out laughing.

But I controlled myself.

"Thank you, Mrs. Harrington," Rosemary said. "But that's okay. In fact, I think I have to be going now. My mom's coming to pick me up soon."

"Oh, I have to go, too," I said.

"Why?" Erica looked disappointed.

"Because I have to ask my mom about skipping ballet on Saturday so I can go to the Little Miss Majorette Baton Twirling Twirltacular."

I knew my mom wouldn't like my missing my ballet lesson. Neither would Madame Linda, who is super strict and sometimes smacks us on the thigh if we don't properly turn it out during *ronde de jambe en l'air* (this used to make my ex-best friend Mary Kay Shiner cry, so she quit coming to Madame Linda's. But then, everything makes Mary Kay Shiner cry, so this was no big surprise).

But Madame Linda's disapproval when I skipped Saturday's lesson would be completely worth it.

Especially if I got to be there when Missy ended up winning one of those giant trophies she'd told us about!

"Mom," I said as soon as I got home. I saw Dad first, sitting at the dining room table, which he uses as his office, grading tests from the computer science class he teaches.

But I knew better than to ask him if it was okay if I skipped ballet class to go to Missy's Little Miss Majorette Baton Twirling Twirltacular on Saturday. Because he would just say, "Fine," like he does about everything.

And it would *seem* fine. Until Mom found out.

And then it would turn out it *wasn't* fine. It was always better to ask Mom first. About *everything*.

"Mom," I said when I found her in her bedroom, putting things in a suitcase. This was so startling — my parents never go anywhere — that I completely forgot what I'd been about to say, and went, "Where are you going?"

"Oh, honey," Mom said, brushing some hair from her eyes. "You know. I told you. Daddy and I are going to Cousin Freddie's wedding at Grandma and Grandpa's house this weekend in San Francisco. Pass me that shirt, will you?"

I passed her one of Dad's shirts, which lay folded on the bed. I'd forgotten that she and Dad were going to Cousin Freddie's wedding. I'd only met my mom's cousin Freddie once, at a family reunion at the country club where my grandma and grandpa on my mom's side live in California. Cousin Freddie had let me and Mark drive his golf cart, even though we weren't really big enough to reach the pedals.

It wasn't our fault we accidentally drove the golf cart onto the tennis courts of the country club. No one had been too happy about this, especially Grandpa, who'd yelled at Cousin Freddie for a long time.

"What is it you wanted to know, Allie?" Mom asked.

"Oh," I said. "Well, Missy Harrington is going to compete in the seventh annual Little Miss Majorette Baton Twirling Twirltacular, middle school division, on Saturday, and I really, really want to go. I know I have ballet that morning, but I promise I'll make up my missed lesson over the summer. Erica and Caroline and Sophie and probably

Rosemary are all going. We think it's important that we go to support Missy, who is suffering from self-esteem issues and hardly has any friends due to her teenage hormones. Also, I think I'll learn positive messages there about teamwork, camaraderie, and the spirit of competitiveness."

I had gotten that last part from a book I'd checked out from the school library about female horse jockeys. There wouldn't be any female horse jockeys at the annual Little Miss Majorette Baton Twirling Twirltacular. But I thought the thing about teamwork and competitiveness sounded good, anyway.

"Twirltacular?" My little brother Kevin looked up from Mom and Dad's bed, where he was reading a fancy furniture catalog that had come in the mail. Kevin likes to collect fancy furniture catalogs. "I want to go to Missy's Twirltacular."

"Well, you're not invited," I said. Kevin was always trying to hang around with my friends. He thought they liked him as much as they liked me, which wasn't true, actually.

"Oh, dear," Mom said. "Is Missy's competition this coming Saturday?"

"Yes," I said. "But I'm sure Uncle Jay won't mind."

"Uncle Jay's not —" Kevin started to say, but Mom interrupted him, even though one of the rules at our house is *Don't interrupt people*.

"Honey, I forgot to tell you," Mom said. "This Saturday is Brittany Hauser's birthday. And she's invited you. And I'm afraid I already told her mother that you'd go."

RULE #2

If You Are Going to Lie to Other People About Why You Aren't Going to Do Something with Them That You Said You Were Going to, You Had Better Make It a Really Good Lie

On the list of worst things that can happen, ever, number one is:

Giant meteor coming down from space and smashing onto Earth, killing everyone on the entire planet, including your parents and your dog and your kitten and your best friends, but for some reason leaving you and Joey Fields, the boy you have to sit next to all day in school, who barks like a dog instead of talking, alive.

Number two is: After the meteor comes down and kills everyone on Earth including your dog and your kitten, except for you and Joey Fields, the only thing left to eat is tomatoes, the food you hate most out of all the foods in the entire world.

Number three is: The meteor also destroys Disney World.

Number four is: Joey Fields still wants you to be his girlfriend, anyway, even though everyone else is dead and he should be busy being consumed with grief and all.

The number five worst thing that could happen is: Brittany Hauser, the meanest girl on the entire planet, who thinks a fun playdate (and who actually uses the *word* "playdate") is to put a live cat in a suitcase and swing it around her head, invites you to her birthday party, and your mother says you can go.

"Mom!" I yelled when I heard this. "Why would you do this? Why would you say that I could go to Brittany Hauser's birthday party without even asking me first? You know I hate her!"

"Now, Allie," Mom said, closing the top of the suitcase. "Don't say hate. You know you don't hate anyone."

Which wasn't true. I hate a lot of people. I hate Brittany Hauser, the meanest girl at my old school. I hate Cheyenne O'Malley, the snobbiest girl at my new school.

I hate people who are mean to animals.

I hate people who start wars.

I hate people (such as Cheyenne O'Malley) who are mean to people who never did anything but be nice to them.

Seriously, that is a lot of hate.

But I didn't say any of that to my mom, who I knew would just tell me to stop being so hateful.

Instead, I said, taking a deep breath and trying to remember to be mature, "Mom. Why would you say I would go to Brittany Hauser's party *without even asking me if I wanted to go first?*"

"Well," Mom said, looking as if she felt a bit guilty. "I'll admit I ought to have done that, Allie, and I do apologize. But you can't tell me you're still upset over that silly fight you and those girls had before we moved. That was so long ago!"

Silly fight? Excuse me, but since when is animal cruelty ever silly? Besides, the last time I'd seen Brittany Hauser, I'd been smashing a cupcake in her face. What was Brittany doing even inviting me to her birthday party, anyway?

"It's just," Mom went on, "that Mrs. Hauser called and asked if I thought you'd want to go, and we got to talking about *Good News!* — she's a big fan of the show, you know. Mr. Hauser's BMW dealership is one of the show's most generous advertisers. And one thing led to another, and she told me about the party, and I said you'd go, and I guess it just slipped my mind."

Slipped her mind? My having to go to the birthday party of my enemy, one of the meanest, bossiest girls in the entire town, just *slipped her mind*?

And okay, it was true my mom was getting to be a very famous celebrity now that she was the film critic for *Good News!*, the local cable entertainment news show.

Well, famous to people like Mrs. Hauser, anyway.

She still wasn't famous enough for us to get into restaurants for free or for me to take a limo to school or anything.

But still.

"Brittany Hauser doesn't even like me," I said. "She only invited me to her stupid party because of *you*, Mom."

Mom blinked at me. "Me? What do you mean?"

"Because you're a celebrity," I said. "You have your own TV show."

"*Good News!* is hardly my own show, Allie," Mom said. "I'm only on it a few times a month, and then only for five minutes. I don't even get paid!"

The fact that my mom doesn't get paid to be on *Good News!* was something my dad brought up a lot. My mom hadn't mentioned that part when she'd said she'd gotten the job. Technically, my dad said, it wasn't even exactly a job. More like volunteer work.

"Well, five minutes a few times a month is more than anybody else's parent we know is on TV," I said, slumping down onto the bed next to Kevin. "It's not fair. I don't want to go to Brittany's stupid party on Saturday. I want to go to the Little Miss Majorette Baton Twirling Twirltacular."

"You might have fun at Brittany's party," Mom said brightly. "You haven't even asked what Brittany's got planned for all of you."

"I can guess," I said, rolling my eyes. "She's going to stick me in a suitcase, then she's going to twirl me around over her head."

"No," Mom said. "Mrs. Hauser is renting a limo and taking all you girls into the city."

I think my eyes must have bulged out of my head. I know Kevin dropped the furniture catalog he'd been holding and sat up.

"Limo?" he yelled. "Allie gets to ride in a *limo*?"

"A BMW SUV limo from Mr. Hauser's dealership," Mom said. "And don't yell. Then Mrs. Hauser is taking all you girls to Glitterati," Mom went on.

"Glitterati?" Kevin yelled. Glitterati is a very famous store in the city where they do nothing but host birthday parties. For girls and for boys, too. You go there and get a makeover (hair and makeup . . . even the boys, if they choose to be a pirate, or something. Like, they put glitter gel in the boys' hair and give them an eye patch or whatever), and then they let you dress up in the costume of your choice. Like, you could be an undercover rock star or a teen superstar or prep school princess. They have everything.

After you have your look put together, you strut down a red carpet runway, and a photographer takes your picture. You don't get to keep the outfit (unless your mom is there to buy it for you), but you get to keep the photo.

Kevin has been wanting to go to Glitterati since the day he was born, practically.

"And when you're through there," Mom went on, "you're going to The Cheesecake Factory for dinner and for Brittany's birthday cake."

"Cheesecake Factory?" I breathed.

I had never been to Glitterati, or to The Cheesecake Factory, because both of these places were very far from our town. They were in the city, which was next to the airport, which was more than an hour away. I had been to the airport, of course, to pick up our relatives when they came to visit.

But the nearest we have ever gotten to The Cheesecake Factory was the Old Spaghetti Factory, which I had actually hated, because practically everything there is to eat at the Old Spaghetti Factory is red. And one of my rules, of course, is Never eat anything red.

"Yes," Mom said. "Then, after dinner, you're going to go stay overnight in the luxury Hilton Hotel downtown, where you'll watch the new Jonas Brothers movie on pay-per-view and order room service in your own suite. Then, in the morning, you'll enjoy brunch in the hotel restaurant —"

"The one with the waterfall and glass elevators in the open-air atrium?" Kevin looked outraged. We had been to the Hilton Hotel once with Mom and Dad when Grandma's plane was late and there was nothing else to do while waiting to pick her up but go into the city and ride the glass elevators at the Hilton up and down.

At least, until the hotel manager had come out and asked us to please go find something else to do, as Kevin's shrieks of delight were disturbing the customers.

"Yes," Mom said. "Then the limo will take you home. But I guess you'd rather go to Missy's baton-twirling thing. I understand."

I sat there with my mouth open. I couldn't believe it: a ride to the city in a real genuine limo, a trip to Glitterati, dinner at The Cheesecake Factory, a night in a luxury hotel suite with room service and pay-per-view movies, brunch in an open-air atrium with a real waterfall and glass elevators . . .

. . . and all I had to do in exchange was put up with bossy Brittany Hauser for twenty-four hours?

It would be totally worth it.

Except . . .

Except what about Missy, and her self-esteem issues, and going to the Little Miss Majorette Baton Twirling Twirltacular with Erica, Caroline, Sophie, and possibly Rosemary to support her?

"I want to go," Kevin said, climbing to his feet. "I'd like to ride in a limo, please. I'd like to go to Glitterati and dress as a pirate, and then stay at the Hilton Hotel."

"You're not invited," Mom said. "And I've told you before, no standing on the bed."

"But Brittany might like me to come," Kevin said. "All of Allie's friends like walking me to school. They think I'm very cute."

"You can't come," I said to Kevin, hitting him in the stomach. Only not hard enough to hurt him. Just hard enough to make him sit down. "Brittany's my friend, not yours. And you're not that cute."

Kevin started to howl, even though I'd barely touched him.

"I want to go!" he shrieked. "I want to go to Glitterati!"

"What's all this yelling in here?" Dad came into the master bedroom. "What about glitter?"

"Allie punched me in the stomach!" Kevin wailed. "I want to ride in a limo!"

"I did not punch him," I said. "I lightly tapped him. And he can't ride in the limo. He's not invited."

"Kevin, she barely touched you," Mom said. "I was standing right here, watching. And you know perfectly well you aren't invited. Take your catalog and go up to your room and add it to your collection."

Kevin, mad that he wasn't invited to Brittany Hauser's

party (which is ridiculous, because Brittany Hauser hardly even knows him), grabbed his catalog and stomped from the room. My other little brother, Mark, happened to walk in at the exact same time, just having gotten back from bike riding with his friends.

"What's with him?" he wanted to know about Kevin.

"Oh, he's just mad," I said. "Because I get to ride in a BMW SUV limo to the city to Glitterati, then go to The Cheesecake Factory, then spend the night in the luxury Hilton Hotel with room service, then have brunch in the open-air atrium and come back in the limo."

"With who?" Mark demanded, looking outraged.

"Brittany Hauser," I said.

Mark stopped looking so outraged. He shuddered and said, "Gross." Then he added, "Glitterati! Glitterati! Ha! Ha! Ha!" Then he left the room, still laughing.

"I suppose," Mom said thoughtfully, "I can get you out of it if you really want me to, Allie. I could tell Mrs. Hauser that I didn't know you'd already made other plans."

I thought about Missy and her sparkly costumes, and of "I'm Gonna Knock You Out." I thought of the twirling trophy, as tall as me, that Missy was hoping to win. I thought of her self-esteem issues, and how important Erica said it was that we be there in the stands, cheering for her on Saturday. I thought of the little bags of popcorn.

I thought of how mean Brittany had been to me the last time I'd been to her house, and what a bad best friend Mary Kay Shiner — who was sure to be at Brittany's party — had been, compared to Erica, Caroline, Sophie, and even Rosemary, who'd started out as someone who wanted to beat me up.

Those guys had always been there for me, whereas Brittany and Mary Kay had only ever made fun of me, at least toward the end of our friendship. They only wanted to be friends with me now because of my mom's celebrity.

But a limo!

This might be my only chance, ever, to ride in a limo.

At least until I was a famous actress slash veterinarian, which was what I planned on being when I grew up.

I thought about the thing with the makeover at Glitterati. And the fact that afterward you walk down a runway, and they take pictures of you. It would probably be good practice for when I'm an actress slash vet. Probably I'd be walking down lots of runways and even red carpets, with photographers snapping pictures of me all the time. If I didn't practice doing that now, at Glitterati, when would I?

"That's okay," I said to Mom. "I'll go to Brittany's stupid party, I guess."

Even as I said it, I felt terrible . . . like I was betraying Erica and her sister and all my friends . . . my really, really good friends.

But the limo! And Glitterati! And The Cheesecake Factory!

"Well," Mom said. "That's settled, then."

"Has it occurred to anyone," Dad said, "that the idea of renting an SUV limo and carting a bunch of girls into the city for dinner and a night in a hotel suite for a tenth birthday party is completely ludicrous, not to mention an utter waste of money?"

"Tom," Mom said. "It's the Hausers' money. They can spend it however they see fit."

"You mean they can flush it down the toilet," Dad said.

"Because that's what they're doing. What are the rest of us supposed to do when it's our daughters' birthdays?" Dad looked down at me. "I suppose you're going to want to go spend the night in a hotel in the city for your birthday, too, now, aren't you?"

"No," I said. "I want a horse for my birthday."

Dad threw his hands up in the air. "You see?" he said to Mom. "You see what they started? Well, I'm staying out of it." Then he went back into the dining room to finish grading papers.

"Well," Mom repeated. "That's settled, then. You'll be going to the party. I'll let Great-Aunt Joyce know she'll only have the boys to look after on Saturday night."

"Wait a minute? Great-Aunt Joyce?" My voice cracked. "That's who's coming to stay with us while you and Dad are at Cousin Freddie's wedding? Great-Aunt *Joyce*? Why not Uncle Jay?"

Mom gave me a very sarcastic look.

"Considering the amount of cake batter I scraped off the kitchen ceiling after the sleepover he supervised," she said, "your uncle Jay is lucky I even let him back inside this house. Your great-aunt Joyce is driving down to stay with you kids this weekend, and I'm not going to hear another word about it."

I almost gagged with disappointment. I wasn't exactly Great-Aunt Joyce's biggest fan. It wasn't just that Great-Aunt Joyce, who is my dad's mom's older sister, was a million years old. There are lots of people who are even older than Great-Aunt Joyce who are way more fun than she is. All Great-Aunt Joyce ever talks about is how she thinks we have way too many toys and how, in her day, all she had to play with were some paper dolls she made herself out of cardboard and two Popsicle sticks.

And when she comes to stay with us, she acts super strict about turning the lights off exactly at nine o'clock, and won't let me read until nine-fifteen, like Dad usually does. She also doesn't believe me about not liking to eat anything red, just like Grandma, and always tries to force me to eat tomatoes, because she says they're "good" for me.

Only how good can they be for me when they make me feel like I'm going to throw up?

"Mom," I said, even though I knew it was completely futile, which means there was no point in trying. "Great-Aunt Joyce smells funny." This is totally true. She smells like medicine. Only maybe that's just because that's what I always end up having to take when she's around, because she makes me so sick. "Plus, she doesn't believe me about how I can't eat tomatoes."

"Stop exaggerating, Allie," Mom said. "Your great-aunt Joyce is a lovely, caring woman. And she won't let you slide down the stairs on mattresses or put cake batter on the ceiling, the way Uncle Jay would. Besides, you won't even be around for twenty-four of the hours that she's here."

This was a cheering thought. Suddenly, I wanted to go to Brittany's party more than ever.

"I just have to figure out a way to tell Erica and those guys," I said thoughtfully. "They're going to be super disappointed that I'm not going with them to the Little Miss Majorette Baton Twirling Twirltacular. We pretty much all agreed we'd go together." I felt a little bit of a pang as I thought about Missy's glittery costumes, all of which

Mrs. Harrington had spent so many hours hand-sewing. "I really did want to see her compete."

"Missy will be in other baton-twirling competitions," Mom said. For some reason there was a note of laughter in her voice. "I'm sure."

"Well," I said. "I hope Erica and those guys will understand."

"Of course they will," Mom said.

But the more I thought about it after I went up to my room, the more I thought maybe my friends *wouldn't* understand. After all, we'd agreed we'd go to the Little Miss Majorette Baton Twirling Twirltacular together and support Missy (well, all of us except Rosemary, who thought twirling was boring).

How was it going to look if I said I wasn't going now because I wanted to ride in a limo to the Glitterati store in the city, have dinner at The Cheesecake Factory, and spend the night in a fancy hotel?

It was going to look like I wanted to spend time with my friends from my old school instead of with them.

Which wasn't true. I didn't even like Brittany Hauser.

But I really, really wanted to have my photo taken on a runway.

The more I thought about it, the more I thought that maybe by saying yes to Brittany Hauser's party invitation, I wasn't being that good of a friend to Erica. After all, I had promised I'd go with her. Sort of.

And here I was, breaking that promise, all because I'd gotten a better invitation from someone I didn't even like that much. Or at all, even.

And *breaking a promise to do something with one person, just because someone else asked you to do something way more exciting, is a rotten thing to do.* That's a rule.

What I needed, I realized, was to come up with a really good story about why I couldn't go to Missy's Little Miss Majorette Baton Twirling Twirltacular. Something that wouldn't be a lie, exactly — because lying was wrong.

Except that *this* lie wouldn't be totally wrong. Because it would be a lie to make other people feel better.

And my saying I was going to a party instead of Missy's twirling competition wasn't going to make anyone feel better. It was only going to make Erica and those guys feel bad that *they* hadn't been invited to Brittany Hauser's party (even though they didn't know her. If they did, they wouldn't feel bad about not being invited to her party, because Brittany is such a stuck-up brat).

What was going to make them feel bad was that I'd chosen to go to Brittany's party instead of hanging out at Missy's Little Miss Majorette Baton Twirling Twirltacular with them.

What was also going to make them feel bad was the fact that they hadn't been invited to ride in a limo to the Glitterati store in the city and to have dinner at The Cheesecake Factory and to spend the night in the Hilton Hotel afterward.

So I had to make up a really, really good lie. One that would make these things not sound so fun.

Because *if you are going to lie to other people about why you aren't going to do something with them that you said you were going to, you had better make it a really good lie.* That's another rule.

So I lay around and thought about my lie for a really long time. I thought about it for most of the rest of the afternoon, all through dinner, and then past homework and TV time and into bath time and getting ready for bedtime.

And then by the time I was about to fall asleep, I had a brilliant idea. I was sure I had come up with the perfect lie.

All I had to do was try it out on Erica and all those guys in the morning.

I was sure it was going to work.

It just had to!

RULE #3

It's Okay to Lie If No One Finds Out You're Lying, and the Lie Doesn't Hurt Anyone, and It Isn't That Big of a Lie, and It's Partially Based on Something True. Sort of

"So the thing is," I said to Erica, Sophie, and Caroline on our way to school the next morning, "I can't go to Missy's Little Miss Majorette Baton Twirling Twirltacular."

"What?" Erica looked crestfallen, which means really sad.

"Why not?" Caroline asked. "Wouldn't your mother let you skip your ballet lesson?"

"Ballet isn't really that good for girls," Sophie said. "Toe shoes are a leading cause of twisted ankles."

"Not if you're properly trained," I said. Sophie was always reading about new ways you could get sick or hurt yourself. If you ask me, she was a little overly concerned about her own health, which is unhealthy. That should be a rule, actually. "And anyway, Madame Linda doesn't let us go on toe shoes until we're twelve."

"But stress fractures can occur in regular ballet shoes," Sophie went on.

"The *point*," I said — sometimes it's very hard to get to the point with my friends, because they are always going off in other directions conversationally, especially Sophie — "is that I can't go to Missy's event, because my mom says I have to go to Brittany Hauser's stupid birthday party instead."

Erica, Caroline, and Sophie gasped. Kevin, who was walking between us on our way to school, sucked in his breath, too.

But that was because I was pretty sure he was going to tell them about Glitterati. So I poked him in the back of the head. Not hard enough to hurt, but hard enough to remind him about the deal we'd made at breakfast: He wouldn't say anything about Brittany's party, and I would give him all my dessert for the rest of the week. This was part of the plan I'd come up with the night before.

"That's terrible!" Erica cried. "Brittany Hauser?"

"Who's Brittany Hauser?" Caroline asked.

"You remember, Caroline," Erica said. "She's that horrible girl from Allie's old school who likes to put cats in suitcases and then shake them around."

"She sounds just like someone else we know," Sophie said. "Whose initials start with *C* and *O*."

She meant Cheyenne O'Malley. Only I had never known Cheyenne O'Malley to be cruel to animals. Just other girls.

"Brittany Hauser is rich," Kevin said, because he couldn't control himself. "You should see her house. It's practically a mansion. They have real marble floors and a swimming pool. With a slide!"

I squeezed the back of Kevin's neck as a warning sign that he better not say anything else.

"Oh, I remember you telling us about her," Caroline said. "She's horrible! Why would you go to her party when you could come with us to see Missy twirl?"

"Yeah," Sophie said. "What about Missy's terrible self-esteem problem? I'm afraid this will be another blow to her, from which she may never recover."

I sort of doubted that. I sort of doubted Missy had any self-esteem problems at all. But I didn't say so out loud. Instead, I said, "I know. And I'm really sorry."

This was the part where I had to tell the big lie. I had been practicing it all morning in the mirror, and I was ready. At least, I was pretty sure I was ready.

"The thing is, I don't want to go to Brittany's party," I said. "But you know Brittany's dad owns the BMW dealership in town, and he pays for a lot of the ads on my mom's show, *Good News!*"

"Yeah?" Caroline already sounded like she didn't approve of what she was hearing.

But I went on, anyway. This was probably one of the biggest lies I had ever told.

But it wasn't exactly untrue. It was just slightly exaggerated.

"And my mom said if I didn't go to Brittany's party, Mr. Hauser might be mad and pull his advertisements from the show. And then *Good News!* could lose a lot of money."

Of course my mom had never said any such thing. But I had seen this sort of thing happen on an episode of a TV show. It definitely *could* happen.

Just not to me. Or my mom. Or *Good News!*

Sophie gasped. "Oh, my goodness!" she cried. "Allie, that's horrible!"

"That . . . that is so mean!" Erica looked completely flabbergasted. "It's . . . it's like . . . it's like he's *buying friends* for Brittany!"

"It really is," Caroline agreed soberly. "I've never heard of something so sad. It almost makes me feel sorry for poor Brittany Hauser. Talk about self-esteem issues."

"Uh," I said. "You don't have to feel sorry for Brittany. Remember the suitcase thing?"

"Yes," Caroline said. "But now we know why she did that. What kind of parents does she have?"

Well, the truth was, Brittany's parents had actually been really mad at her when they'd found out about Brittany putting Lady Serena Archibald in the suitcase. Her mom had grounded her for a really long time. . . .

"Oh, Allie!" Erica flung her arms around me. "I'm so sorry! I can't believe you have to go to that horrible girl's birthday party. It's going to be so terrible. I don't know if I'm going to be able to have fun while I'm watching Missy, thinking about you at that awful birthday party."

"It's okay," I said. Erica was practically strangling me, she was hugging me so hard. "You can still have a good time watching Missy. I'll be all right. I'm a very strong person."

"I don't know," Sophie said. "What are they going to be making you do at Brittany's party, anyway? Please don't say it's going to be one of those awful grown-up parties where they make you dress up in a scratchy party dress and shiny shoes and go to the country club with all the adults."

"Oh, I went to one of those once for my cousin," Caroline said, making a face. "It was terrible! Is it going to be like that, Allie?"

"It's not going to be like that at all," Kevin burst out, because he just couldn't help it anymore.

"Uh, never mind him," I said, escaping Erica's grip and moving toward Kevin to lay a hand on the back of his neck so I could squeeze it a little again. "Kevin, why don't you go play on the jungle gym?"

"Allie gets to ride in a limo," Kevin said, his voice sounding strangled, because I was squeezing slightly more tightly with his every word. "To Glitterati! And then to The Cheesecake Factory for dinner, and then to the luxury Hilton Hotel downtown, where they're going to watch pay-per-view movies and order room service all night, then have brunch in the open-air atrium by the glass elevators near the waterfall!"

I gave Kevin a tiny push toward the jungle gym, where the other kindergartners were gathered doing their little kindergartner business.

"Good-bye, Kevin," I said. "Have a fun day at school."

"Bye," he said, staggering away, even though I really hadn't pushed him that hard. Much.

"Wow," Caroline said, watching Kevin go. "That's some birthday party."

"That doesn't sound so bad," Erica said, brightening. "Glitterati! That seems like a fun birthday party. Why do you look so sad about it, Allie?"

"Well," I said, "because I'd rather spend the day with you guys, of course, at Missy's Twirltacular."

This was a lie. But it wasn't entirely a lie. I *would* rather have spent the day with them. In a limo, and at Glitterati.

"Aw," Erica said, moving in to hug me again. "Allie, that's so sweet! But I'm happy you get to do all those fun things. It's such a relief. I thought you were going to have a terrible time with that Brittany girl. But it sounds like you're going to have a great time."

"Yeah," Sophie said. "I've never even gotten to do one of those things during a birthday party. Let alone *all* of them at *one* birthday party."

"Well," I said, feeling a little uncomfortable. Not just because I'd lied to them, but because Erica was still hugging me really hard. "Like Kevin said. Brittany Hauser is very rich."

"I feel sorry for her," Erica said, finally letting me go.

"Look what she did to that cat. That's a sign of an unhappy person, no matter how much money she has."

"And you can see where she gets it from. Her dad, threatening to pull his advertising money if Allie doesn't come to his daughter's party?" Caroline shook her head. "That's messed up."

"It's like the evil warlord," Erica said, talking about our made-up game of queens, "trying to pour hot oil on us all because Sophie won't marry him."

"Really," Sophie agreed. "I can't believe your mom is putting up with it, Allie."

"Well," I said. My lie was getting to be a little bit bigger than I had meant it to be. "It's not like she has a choice. She could lose her job."

Sophie gasped. "And then your parents won't have enough money to pay your bills! Like your medical bills, if someone gets sick."

I didn't want to admit that my mom wasn't even getting paid for being on *Good News!* That made her seem like less of a celebrity. Whoever heard of someone who was on TV but didn't even get paid for it?

"My mom would still have her other job," I pointed out. "She works as an adviser at the same college where my dad teaches computer classes. Remember?"

"Right," Erica said. "Hey, you guys. In a way, Allie is just like Sophie, torn between the warlord and Prince Peter. Allie's torn between us and her mom and Mr. Hauser!"

"Only Prince Peter is way nicer than Brittany Hauser," Sophie pointed out, glancing at the boy she'd had a crush on since forever, Peter Jacobs, who was playing kick ball over on the baseball diamond with Rosemary and my brother Mark and a bunch of other people. Today Peter was wearing a bright yellow sweater. He looked very handsome in it, as usual.

"Um," I said. "Yeah. I guess." I couldn't believe how easily they'd believed my lie. I'd gotten out of having to go to Missy's Twirltacular, and Erica and Caroline and Sophie weren't mad at me. They even felt sorry for me!

And I was the one who was getting to go to the Glitterati store in a limo, and stay overnight in the city in a hotel. . . .

This was turning out to be the best lie ever.

And okay . . . I did feel a little bit guilty. But . . .

It's okay to lie if no one finds out you're lying, and the lie doesn't hurt anyone, and it isn't that big of a lie, and it's partially based on something true. Sort of. That's a rule.

Of course, I still wanted to go to Missy's Little Miss Majorette Baton Twirling Twirltacular.

On the other hand . . . Missy herself would probably rather be riding in a limo into the city to do all the fun things I was going to get to be doing. I mean, let's face it . . . it wasn't every day you got to go to Glitterati or to eat in a fancy restaurant like The Cheesecake Factory or stay overnight in a place like the Hilton Hotel downtown.

Missy, I was sure, would understand. Anyone would.

So my lie was perfectly understandable. It barely even counted as a lie. It was practically the truth.

Sort of.

RULE #4

In My House, Nothing Will Get You in Bigger Trouble than Lying

It started raining hard that morning, which meant we had to stay inside Room 209 for recess, which I sometimes like because it means Mrs. Hunter gets out her old board games from when she was a kid and lets us play with them.

Her games are very old-fashioned and make us laugh, such as the Game of Life, which is Erica's favorite, which has little cars for game pieces. The cars move along a board with a wheel you spin that tells you how many spaces you can move your car. Inside your car are little holes you can fill up with pink and blue pegs — the Mom and Dad and their babies, as Erica calls them.

All Erica wants to do is fill up her car with as many pegs as she can, even though that's not the point of the game (having a career and making money is).

But Erica just wants to have a car full of little pink and blue pegs.

The game I like is Clue. It's a murder mystery game. It's my favorite, but the only other person in our class who likes it is Joey Fields.

Sophie says Clue is morbid. Sophie's favorite game is Monopoly. That's a game where you try to own as much property as you can, and if someone's game piece lands on your property, they have to pay you. I hate this game more than any game ever invented, even more than I hate Boggle, which is a word search game of Mrs. Hunter's that no one likes but Caroline.

The only game that all of my friends will agree to play together is the Game of Life (even though Erica won't play it right).

We were playing the Game of Life — even Rosemary agreed to play, though usually she plays indoor finger football with the boys — when Cheyenne O'Malley walked up to us with her good friends Marianne and Dominique (or M and D as she likes to call them) behind her and said, "So, Allie. I understand that you're taking a limo to Glitterati."

I was busy achieving great things in the Game of Life, so I didn't really have time to talk to Cheyenne.

"Yeah, so?" I said, spinning the wheel.

"So, I just think you should know," Cheyenne said. "Glitterati is for babies."

"No, it's not," Rosemary said, not looking up from the game board. "I heard a girl in fifth grade went there for her birthday party last month. So you're wrong, Cheyenne."

"And for someone who is super concerned about acting mature," Caroline added, "you're sure not acting like it at the moment, Cheyenne."

Cheyenne's face turned a delicate shade of pink that matched the pegs in Erica's car.

"Well," she said, "I guess you think you're so great, don't you, Allie, because you get to ride in a limo, and eat at The Cheesecake Factory, and stay in a fancy hotel this weekend."

"She doesn't even want to go," Erica said, looking up from her little car crammed full of passengers. "She wants to go to my sister Missy's Twirltacular. Her mom is *making* her go to Brittany Hauser's birthday party. If Allie doesn't go, her mom could get fired from *Good News!*"

Hmmm. This wasn't going quite the way I'd planned. Soon a lot more people than I'd thought were going to know about my lie.

"Well," Cheyenne said. "Just so you know, if you're going to a party where the girl's parents are taking you out to dinner and to Glitterati and all that, you better make sure the cost of the gift you're giving her is equal to or more than the amount her parents are spending on you. I'm only telling you this," Cheyenne added, "because you're so immature, I'm sure you don't know it already, Allie. I'm trying to *help* you."

Rosemary slammed her fist down onto the Game of Life game board, making everyone's game pieces jump. Then she stood up slowly.

"None of us," she said, looking Cheyenne straight in the eye, "needs 'help' like yours, Cheyenne."

"Speak softly to your neighbors, please," Mrs. Hunter called from her desk, where she was sitting preparing a lesson. We all looked over and saw that Mrs. Hunter was staring at us with her green eyes crackling . . .

. . . which is exactly what you *didn't* want from Mrs. Hunter, who was the prettiest, nicest teacher I'd ever had, and who'd once told my grandma that I was a joy to have around the classroom.

But Mrs. Hunter could be very scary when she got angry.

We lowered our voices immediately.

Cheyenne, who had to tilt her head a little to look Rosemary in the eye because Rosemary was so much taller than she was, seemed a bit scared. And not of Mrs. Hunter.

"Whatever," Cheyenne whispered. "I was only trying to be a friend. That's all. Geez."

Cheyenne and her two pals M and D slunk back to their desks, where they were busy doing what they usually did on rainy days: drawing fairies with Mrs. Hunter's collection of glitter gel pens (which I did, too, sometimes, when I wasn't busy drawing zombies to show Stuart Maxwell that I could, or playing the Game of Life).

"Don't listen to her, Allie," Caroline said after Cheyenne had left. "You don't have to get Brittany a huge, expensive gift, no matter how much her parents are paying for her party."

"Right," Sophie said. "Remember for your birthdays last year, Caroline and Erica, I made you each photo albums of pictures of us together?"

"I loved that!" Erica smiled. "You scrapbooked that cover for it using funny things we used to say last summer."

" 'Hey, you in the yellow swim trunks,' " Caroline said.

" 'I'll have another doughnut, please. No, I'll have two!' " Sophie cried.

Caroline dissolved into giggles — which was unusual for her, since Caroline wasn't a giggler. "Remember Little Hiawatha?"

Sophie screamed politely.

"I was so sure we were going to get caught!" Erica said.

"Girls!" Mrs. Hunter said. "Please keep it down. We don't want Mrs. Danielson coming in here, now do we?"

"No, ma'am," Rosemary said. She glared at Erica, Caroline, and Sophie, who were crying, they were laughing so hard. "You guys," Rosemary said. "Shut up. It isn't that funny."

Seriously. It wasn't that funny. Rosemary and I had no idea who Little Hiawatha was, or why the mention of him — or the boy in yellow swim trunks, or the thing with the doughnuts — should make Erica, Sophie, and Caroline laugh so hard.

To tell the truth, it sort of made me feel left out. This made me worry about other things I was going to feel left out of. Like Missy's Twirltacular. Were they going to come home from that with all sorts of private jokes, like the Little Hiawatha one, that I wasn't going to understand?

Maybe I'd made a mistake choosing to go to Brittany's birthday party instead.

And that was the other thing: I couldn't make a lovely photo album (because I didn't even have any photos of myself with her) to give to Brittany Hauser on her birthday. I didn't even have any private jokes with Brittany Hauser (unless you counted the fact that she'd put her mom's cat in a suitcase and shook it around and I'd told on her and she'd tortured me about it for weeks afterward by calling me Allie Stinkle).

Because she and I weren't even that good friends. We were frenemies, really. Which is a mix of friends and enemies. We'd started out friends, then become enemies, then she'd tried to become my friend, then I'd shoved a cupcake in her face.

And now, for some reason, she was still trying to be my friend.

I was sort of starting to regret saying I'd go to Brittany's party.

Especially when I went home for lunch that day and yelled from the mudroom (which, for once, really was filled with mud, because it was raining so hard, Kevin and I got soaked walking from school), "Mom! What did you get for me to give to Brittany for her birthday? We have to give her something super good. Because Cheyenne O'Malley says you have to get something that costs equal to or more than whatever Brittany's parents are spending on what I'm going to eat and drink at the party, not to mention the cost of my going to Glitterati and however much it's going to cost for me to spend the night at the Hilton Hotel. . . . Mom? *Mom?*"

But there was no response from Mom. Just . . . nothing.

Which was weird. Because she and Dad weren't supposed to leave for the airport until later that night.

I followed Kevin into the kitchen, where Mark was already standing. He'd gotten home before us, since he'd ridden his bike . . . but that meant he was more soaked. He hadn't even gone upstairs to change out of his sopping wet clothes yet, he was just standing there making a big puddle on the kitchen floor. At first I had no idea why.

Until I saw that he was staring at Mom. Mom, who was on the phone by the kitchen counter, with a very worried expression on her face. She was going, "Uh-huh. Of course. I understand. Oh, I'm so sorry. I'm just so sorry."

What had happened? Clearly something very, very bad. Mom looked awful. Her face was pale and she was holding the phone so tightly, her knuckles were white.

I knew right away that something had gone wrong.

And I knew what it was, too.

My lie. My lie about how Mom was making me go to Brittany Hauser's party had been found out.

I didn't know who had told. Probably no one had done it maliciously (which means on purpose and to be evil). It had probably just slipped out.

And now I was going to get in big trouble. I would probably be grounded and I wouldn't be able to go to Brittany's party *or* to the annual Little Miss Majorette Baton Twirling Twirltacular.

Of course, I had brought it all on myself. But still. It wasn't fair. I had only been trying to spare my friends' feelings. It hadn't been a lie to hurt anyone. I had done it so as *not* to hurt anyone.

I stood there in the kitchen trying to figure out what to do. Should I go to my room now, before my mom could send me there? Surely she'd let me have lunch first. My parents had never let me starve before. What was going to happen? Who was that on the phone? Mr. Hauser? Was my mom going to get fired? Could you get fired from a job you weren't paid for? Probably, since my mom had had to audition for it in the first place.

I couldn't believe how much trouble I was in. My mom really liked that job. And Harmony, Uncle Jay's girl-friend, really liked my mom's job, too. She was trying to get a summer internship with Lynn Martinez, the news anchor at the station that showed *Good News!* Now, because of me, that wouldn't happen, either.

I had ruined *everything*.

I couldn't lie about it, either. The one thing my parents hate more than anything in the world is lying. You can pretty much do whatever you want in my house, and you'll get in trouble for it, sure.

But in my house, nothing will get you in bigger trouble than lying. That's a rule. My parents can't stand lying.

So though it might have seemed like a good idea to make up some big excuse about why I'd lied to Erica and Caroline and Sophie about my mom's job being on the line if I didn't go to Brittany's party, I didn't, because she already looked like she was in a bad mood . . . a bad enough mood that if I didn't just confess, she might kill me on the spot.

"Mom," I said, as soon as she hung up. "Listen. I can explain —"

Mom reached up and pushed some of her hair from her face.

"Not now, Allie. That," Mom said, "was your great-aunt Joyce. She threw out her back giving her cat, Mr. Tinkles, a bath. So now she won't be coming to stay while your dad and I are at my cousin Freddie's wedding. . . ."

I closed my mouth. So, that *hadn't* been Lynn Martinez or Mr. Hauser on the phone with my mom? No one had found out about my big lie? I was actually . . . safe?

There was a beat while we all held our breath. . . . Did this mean Mom and Dad wouldn't be going to Cousin Freddie's wedding? Or . . .

"I guess your uncle Jay will be staying with you instead," Mom finished.

Mark, Kevin, and I all looked at one another. It was really hard, but we restrained an urge to high-five one another. Even though we were all sorry for Great-Aunt Joyce and the pain she was going through, hearing this was like hearing that Christmas and our birthdays had all come at once. Uncle Jay was staying with us for a whole weekend, instead of Great-Aunt Joyce? It was truly a miracle. Whatever had happened to make Great-Aunt Joyce throw out her back while giving Mr. Tinkles a bath (and who gave cats baths? I could understand it if the cat was an outdoor cat who got into a fight with a skunk or something. But Mr. Tinkles is an indoor cat . . . and not a show cat like Lady Serena Archibald), it could not have happened to someone who deserved it more. I mean, why make someone eat tomatoes when they make her feel like she is choking? That is nothing but mean.

"It's not funny," Mom said, seeing our smiles. "Great-Aunt Joyce is a very kind person."

Um . . . not really, Mom.

But you can't always change moms' minds about things.

"And don't think it's going to be like last time Uncle Jay stayed over," Mom went on. "There will be no hide-and-seek in the dark with bicycle lights on your heads. There will be no Hot Pockets morning, noon, and night. I am going to have someone look in on you to make sure you kids are being fed properly."

This made us curious. Because I am the oldest, and naturally it is my job to do these things, I asked, "Who?"

Mom was already flipping through her address book.

"Harmony, of course," she said.

RULE #5

Liars Don't Get Any of Harmony's Home-baked Cookies. Unless They Cry Hard Enough

Having a bachelor uncle take care of you for a weekend —
even with his super pretty, highly responsible girlfriend
looking in on you from time to time — is practically like
being an orphan. Everyone knows this. When I got back
to school and told people about it, word got around fast.

"But what are you going to eat?" Elizabeth Pukowski
wanted to know.

"Oh, probably pizza," I told her. "Uncle Jay is a pizza
delivery person for Pizza Express. He gets all the pizza he
wants for free. So that's what we'll probably eat."

"You can't have pizza for breakfast," Elizabeth said. It was still raining, so we were inside for recess again. Mrs. Hunter was back at her desk, not looking too happy about the situation. I didn't blame her. Rosemary had had to drag Patrick Day down from his desk three times already.

"Duh," Dominique said. "They can have cereal for breakfast."

"How come my little sister, Daniella," Marianne, who had been quiet for a surprisingly long time, suddenly piped up to ask, "who's in kindergarten with your little brother Kevin, says that that whole thing about your mom making you go to that girl Brittany's party isn't even true, Allie?"

"What?" I stared at Marianne in horror. It didn't seem like she could possibly have said what I thought she'd just said. Could she have?

Everyone else, I noticed — well, of the girls in Room 209, anyway — was staring at her, too.

"That's what your brother Kevin told my sister," Marianne said. "He told my sister that you made up the thing about Mr. Hauser pulling all his advertising from *Good News!* if you don't go to his daughter's birthday party.

64

You're going to the party just because you want to ride in a limo and go to Glitterati and spend the night in a fancy hotel. That's what my sister says your brother says, anyway."

Oh, no. I wanted to curl up into a ball and die.

"That's not true," Erica said, in a defensive voice. "Allie wants to go to my sister's baton-twirling competition."

"Well," Marianne said. "That's not what Daniella says. She says she made up that whole lie about her mom just so you guys wouldn't be mad at her."

Erica, Caroline, and Sophie looked at me with surprise. Even Rosemary seemed kind of shocked.

"Allie," Rosemary said. "That's not right, is it? You wouldn't lie about going with a bunch of prissy girls you don't even like to that stupid Glitterati store, would you?"

If there was going to be a time to confess that I'd been lying — lying to my best friends, lying to my mom, lying to everyone, basically — about going to that party, this would have been a good time to do it. Maybe I could have said something like, "Well, you see, you guys, the truth is,

I didn't want to hurt your feelings about wanting to go to Glitterati in a limo. So I made up the thing about my mom."

But I didn't. Instead, I used some of my acting skills.

The thing is, I want to be an actress when I grow up. Well, an actress slash veterinarian.

I have been told by a number of people that I am a very good actress. I don't mean to be a braggart, but when I starred in our school play, I was one of the best ones, practically.

So I was pretty confident that acting could help me get out of this situation.

"No," I said, opening my eyes as wide as they would go. "I told you guys. I don't know why Kevin would say that. Except . . . well, Mom didn't tell him the truth about her job thing, of course, because he's too young to know about it, and she doesn't want him to worry. And he's really jealous of me getting to go tomorrow, because he wants to go to Glitterati more than anything in the world. You know how much he loves pirates."

Erica, Sophie, and Caroline exchanged glances. At first, I thought they weren't going to believe me.

But then I saw that they were all nodding, like, *Oh, of course!* They completely believed me.

My acting had totally convinced them.

It convinced Marianne, too. And Rosemary. Everyone in my whole class was like, "Uh-huh," and "That makes sense."

I am seriously the best actress in the fourth grade. Possibly the world.

When I got home from school that afternoon, Mom and Dad were gone, and Uncle Jay and his girlfriend, Harmony, were on the couch in the family room, watching the music video channel we aren't allowed to watch and eating microwave popcorn.

"Hey, kid," Uncle Jay said when he saw me. "What's happening?"

"Nothing," I said. "Where's Kevin?"

"Hi, Allie," Harmony said. She looked all pretty with her straight shiny black hair. "How was school?"

"Fine," I said. "Where's Kevin?"

"I think he's in his room," Uncle Jay said. "Why?"

"No reason," I said. I put down my stuff in a big pile on the kitchen counter, even though when Mom's home we have to put everything away neatly in the cubby marked with our name in the mudroom, or hang it on the peg under our name.

But Mom wasn't home.

"Would you like some popcorn?" Harmony got up from the couch to ask. "Or homemade chocolate chip cookies? I spent all afternoon baking them. Well, they aren't homemade, exactly. They're the kind you buy frozen and then drop on a sheet —"

"I ate most of the dough," Uncle Jay called from the TV room. "It's wrong what they say about eating raw eggs mixed in dough. I must have had about twenty and I feel fine."

Normally, I would never give up home-baked chocolate chip cookies.

But normally, I didn't have something this important to do.

"No, thanks," I said.

I went up the stairs and saw that Kevin's door was closed. He was listening to the soundtrack to the musical *Annie* and practicing his vocals for when *Annie* comes to town and one of the girls playing an orphan gets sick and they need someone to take her place and for some reason there is no girl available to take her part (such as me), and so Kevin has to step in (he told me all about this, even though I said, "Kevin, this is never going to happen").

I threw open his door without knocking (we aren't allowed to have locks on our doors, for reasons of safety).

Kevin was on his bed. When he saw me, he rolled into a ball and screamed, "I didn't do it! I didn't do it!"

This was how I knew he had, indeed, done it.

"You did, too!" I yelled, and jumped onto his bed. "And after I promised to give you all my dessert! You're going to die now. I'm going to kill you!"

I proceeded to sit on Kevin. I didn't care that he was so much smaller than I was. Kevin deserved to die.

"Help!" Kevin screamed. "Help! Help! Uncle Jay! She's killing me!"

About five seconds later, Mark came into the room. He stood there going, "Allie's killing Kevin! Allie's killing Kevin! Uncle Jay, come quick! Allie's killing Kevin!"

Of course, I wasn't really killing Kevin. I was only sitting on him, and even then not very hard.

But this was only because Kevin kept getting away. It is really hard to sit on a kindergartner because they're so squirmy and difficult to get a grip on. Kevin wouldn't keep still long enough for me to properly sit on him. I actually don't know how Missy does it when she sits on one of us and manages to pin us down. She must have very superior sitting skills. I would barely get on top of Kevin before he'd slither away. He kept rolling out from under me. It was like he was a circus performer or something.

I think it was all those dance and gymnastic classes Kevin kept insisting Mom and Dad enroll him in at the Y.

"Allie!" Uncle Jay finally showed up in the doorway. He grabbed me under the armpits and pulled me off Kevin. Kevin wiggled up onto his feet and stood there by his bed laughing because I hadn't been able to really get all my weight on top of him, let alone pin his arms down and spit in his face.

Then, when he saw how scared Uncle Jay looked, he started fake crying.

"Ow," Kevin cried. "Allie sat on me! She weighs a lot!"

"I did not," I yelled, darting forward. "I never got a chance because you kept moving! But I will now, you little tattletale —"

Uncle Jay grabbed my arm and pulled me back.

"Hey, now," he said. "Calm down, calm down. What's this all about?"

"Kevin told a secret he promised not to tell," I said. "And now the whole school knows. Including all my friends!"

"It's not my fault," Kevin said. "I'm just a little kid. How was I supposed to know better than to tell?"

"I promised to give you my dessert for a week in exchange for not telling!" I yelled. "You knew well enough to ask for that, you should have known well enough to keep your mouth shut!"

"It's not my fault," Kevin shouted again as I broke free from Uncle Jay's grasp and started after him again. "I only told Daniella. How was I supposed to know she'd blab it to the whole world?"

"She didn't blab it to the whole world," I yelled. "Just her sister, who's in my class, and now everyone in my class knows. You're lucky all my friends don't hate me!"

"They didn't look like they hated you," Mark said from where he was leaning in the doorway enjoying the whole fight, since he wasn't in it, "when I passed all of you on my bike while you were walking home from school together just now."

"I said he's *lucky* they all don't hate me now," I said. "It was only because of my superior acting skills that I was able to get them to believe me and not Kevin."

"Why?" Harmony wanted to know. She had come up the stairs, too, and was standing there staring at us with a puzzled look on her face, holding a plate of slightly burned chocolate chip cookies. "What are you talking about?"

I put my hands down. It was pointless trying to kill Kevin now that he'd hidden behind Uncle Jay. I would never be able to get at Kevin now. It was three against one, with Uncle Jay and Harmony defending him.

"Nothing," I said. I knew if I told Harmony about my big lie — the one about how Mom was making me go to Brittany Hauser's birthday party tomorrow instead of Erica's sister's baton-twirling competition, or Mr. Hauser would pull all the advertising from *Good News!* — she would never understand. Even though it was a lie for a good cause — to keep Erica's feelings from being hurt — it was just too big a lie for most adults to forgive. They would look right past the part about not wanting to hurt Erica's feelings, and right at the part where I'd told a big fat lie.

I could see Kevin giving me the evil eye from behind Uncle Jay. If he said anything to make me look bad in front of Harmony . . .

But he didn't. He just glared at me.

And then Uncle Jay was squatting down in front of him until his face was the same level as Kevin's. "Are you upset that Allie gets to ride in a limo to a fancy hotel, and she didn't ask you to come with her? Is that why you ratted her out, even though she promised to give you her dessert for a week not to, little dude?"

"Yes," Kevin said, looking like he was going to cry for real now. But mostly, I think, over the idea that he was missing out on all that great stuff.

Uncle Jay shook his head. Then he said, "You shouldn't have done that." He stood up straight and looked at me. "And *you* shouldn't have tried to kill your brother. You were both wrong. Now shake hands."

I didn't want to shake Kevin's hand. He was my enemy.

Harmony cleared her throat. Uncle Jay looked over at her.

"I don't think a handshake is enough," she said meaningfully. "I think maybe they both need to learn a lesson for what they've done. Like . . . they don't get any of my home-baked cookies."

Hearing that, Kevin's eyes filled with great big baby tears . . . and completely spilled over. He let out one of the wails he'd been practicing for when *Annie* comes to town and needs some extra orphans.

"Oh!" Harmony cried in alarm, hastily passing the plate of cookies over toward Kevin. "I'm sorry! You can have some cookies. I'm sure you're sorry for what you did. Right, Allie?"

Sometimes having a little brother who is almost as big a drama queen as my friends comes in handy.

"He's sorry," I said, taking one of the burned cookies as she passed the plate toward me.

On the other hand, he was crying — for real — like he was genuinely sorry for what he'd done.

Or genuinely sorry he wasn't going to get to ride in a limo to Glitterati.

In any case, it is the responsibility of the oldest child to set an example for the youngest ones.

So I stuck out my right hand, and Kevin stuck out his, and we shook hands.

"I'm sorry, Allie," Kevin said, looking like he meant it.

"I'm sorry, too," I said.

I even meant it.

Not sorry that I'd sat on him, though. He'd deserved that. I was just sorry I'd trusted him.

"That's what I like to see," Uncle Jay said. "Now, who wants to go to Pizza Express and make their own pizza?"

We all stared at him.

"That's right," he said. "I've got an in at the restaurant, you know. And my boss said it was all right for you three to come in and make your own pizzas. You can twirl them in the air and everything. I figured it was better for you to get dough on the ceiling there than here."

Really. Uncle Jay is the coolest relative in the world.

I was sad for Great-Aunt Joyce throwing out her back and all.

But having an uncle who dates girls who make cookies and works in a place where they let us make our own pizzas?

That was just the best.

RULE #6

A Present Should Come from the Heart

The next morning I wasn't in a much better mood than the day before, despite having gotten to make my own pizza in a real restaurant kitchen. Mom had left a note that said, since the limo was coming for me at noon, I still had to go to my ballet lesson with Madame Linda at ten o'clock.

Who could concentrate on ballet when a limo was coming to pick them up and take them to Glitterati?

It was horrible to have to stand there in a boring black leotard and pink tights and do *battement tendus* and pliés at the barre with the rest of the class when all I could think about was how I was going to be leaving for Glitterati in two hours! Madame Linda had to slap my thigh three times because I wasn't concentrating on my turn-out (and pardon me, but that hurt)!

And at the end of the class, when we did *révérence*, I did not get to wear Madame Linda's tiara (no surprise). A couple of the girls asked me why I was in such a rush to get out of there when I was jamming my shoes and leg warmers into my backpack, and I got to say, all casual, "Oh . . . a limo is coming to my house to pick me up to take me to Glitterati."

At first they were all, "No way," but then I explained it was for a birthday party, so they were pretty excited for me.

That got me feeling pretty good . . .

. . . until Uncle Jay was pulling into the driveway for home, and I saw Erica and her family, along with Sophie and Caroline, all getting into the Harringtons' minivan to go to Missy's Twirltacular. Erica and Caroline and Sophie saw me and smiled and waved. I waved back. I couldn't open the window because it was raining kind of hard. But I think Caroline and Sophie and Erica all yelled, "Have fun!"

Then they got into the van, all giggling and poking one another and having fun, and shut the door. Then Erica's dad drove away.

And that was that.

Except that it was kind of like they'd closed the door on my going with them.

And I couldn't help feeling like I had made a terrible mistake.

Only I hadn't. Right? I mean, who wouldn't rather go to Glitterati in a limo than to a gymnastics contest in a minivan? Um, hello. Me.

As soon as Uncle Jay stopped the car, I got out of it and ran upstairs to put on my best party clothes (purple shirt, jean miniskirt, yellow leggings, and orange cowboy boots) and try to get into a party mood. I put on some dance music and danced around my room, scaring my adorable kitten Mewsie, who crawled under the bed.

But when I looked in the mirror, I realized the party clothes and dancing hadn't done any good. I was still regretting not going with Erica and those guys to see Missy perform at the Little Miss Majorette Baton Twirling Twirltacular. The first events were due to start any minute.

And I wasn't going to be there to support Missy. Or to enjoy any of the delicious popcorn they'd be serving to the spectators in the middle school gym. Or to see any of the amazing twirlers, coming from as far away as out of state, in their beautiful twirling costumes, all competing for a chance to win golden trophies as big as me.

I mean, yes, I was going to get to ride in a limo, and go to Glitterati, and do all this other stuff I've always wanted to do.

But all of a sudden, the closer it got to the time for me to go, the less fun the idea of going seemed to get.

What was *wrong* with me? All of my dreams were coming true! I was about to get to ride in a limo!

"So, have you got everything?" Uncle Jay asked as I came down the stairs, dragging my overnight wheelie bag behind me, *thump, thump, thump*, one step at a time. "Your toothbrush, your pajamas, some clothes for tomorrow?"

"Yes," I answered. Kevin and Mark were pushing all the furniture in the living room back to make space for our family tent. Since Kevin was so upset about me getting to ride in the limo and stay in a luxury hotel, Uncle Jay had said they could have "boys' time" while I was gone. "Boys' time" meant they got to set up our family tent in the living room (since it was so wet outside) and pretend that they were world explorers, then watch adventure movies and eat adventure food, the kind you could only cook over an outdoor fire, such as campfire beans and hot dogs.

Only Uncle Jay had said they could cook them in the fireplace in the living room instead of outside.

I wondered what Harmony was going to say about this when she stopped by to check in.

"Good," Uncle Jay said. "What about your present for the birthday girl?"

I stared at Uncle Jay blankly. "Didn't Mom leave that with you?" I asked.

Uncle Jay looked back at me just as blankly.

"No," he said. "She just left me a hundred bucks to feed you all."

"She didn't say where Brittany's present was?" I could feel something rising in my throat. What I felt was panic. I'd been right: Deciding to go to this party had been a terrible idea. "I can't go to Brittany's party without a present!"

"Hold on, hold on," Uncle Jay said, reaching into his pocket and pulling out his cell phone. "I'm sure it's around here somewhere. Let me call your mom and ask her."

Uncle Jay dialed the number for my mom's cell phone, while I stood at the bottom of the stairs, icy fear gripping me. What if my mom forgot to buy a present for Brittany? I couldn't go. I wouldn't be able to show my face at Brittany's party if I didn't have a present that cost equal to or more than the cost of the food I would consume at the party. Not to mention however much it would cost for my picture at Glitterati, or my share of however much a room was at the Hilton Hotel —

"Oh, hi, Liz?" Uncle Jay was saying into his phone. "It's Jay — no, no, the kids are fine. Yeah. No, it's still raining. Well, drizzling. What are they doing? Oh, we're just about to sit down and play some of those educational board games you left out —"

"Uncle Jay." Mark walked over, carrying one of Mom's Waterford crystal vases she and Dad got as a wedding present. "Where should I put this so it doesn't get broken as we set up camp?"

"Hold on, Liz," Uncle Jay said. He pointed toward the dining room. "In there, champ."

Mark nodded, and carried the vase away.

"So, listen," Uncle Jay said into the phone. "Allie was wondering where you put the gift for Brittany. She's just about to get picked up for the party." Uncle Jay listened for a minute. Then he nodded. Then he handed the phone to me. "She wants to talk to you," he said.

I took the phone from Uncle Jay and pressed it to my ear. "Yes, Mom?" I said.

"Allie, honey," Mom said. She sounded funny. Maybe it was because she was so far away. Or maybe it was because she was staying at her mom and dad's house, and everyone was getting ready for Cousin Freddie's wedding, and someone had stolen a golf cart again and driven it onto the tennis court. In any case, she didn't sound good. "I forgot Brittany's gift."

These were not the words I wanted to hear. They were so not the words I wanted to hear, my throat closed up and for a second I couldn't breathe.

"Mom," I gargled. "No!"

"But, honey, listen," Mom said. "Just tell Brittany that it's my fault, that I forgot, and that I'll drop her gift off next week —"

"Mom." In front of me, Uncle Jay's face began to swim. That's because my eyes had begun to fill with tears. "You don't understand. I can't go to Brittany's party without a present!"

"Yes, you can, honey," Mom said. There were some kind of crashing noises in the background, and I heard a voice yell, "Oh, no. Freddie!" "Oh," Mom said. "I have to go. But, Allie, just explain to Brittany that I had to go out of town for a wedding and that I'll drop her gift off next week. She'll understand, I promise you. I'll talk to you later, sweetie. Bye-bye."

I handed the phone back to Uncle Jay, even though I couldn't see him very well through my tears.

"She hung up," I said. "It doesn't sound like Cousin Freddie's wedding is going very well."

"Big surprise," Uncle Jay said. He didn't know Cousin Freddie, but he knew *of* him. He put his phone back in his pocket. "What did she say to do?"

"She said she'll drop Brittany's present off next week," I said. Now the tears were coming, spilling out of my eyes and trickling down my cheeks. "But you don't understand. I can't go to this party without a present! Not with these kinds of girls. Brittany and her friends . . . they used to call me Allie Stinkle. They'll make fun of me if I don't bring a present."

"Well," Uncle Jay said. "Why do you want to go to a party with a bunch of people like that, anyway?"

This was a very good point. Suddenly, more than anything, I wished I had gotten into that van with everyone going to the Little Miss Majorette Baton Twirling Twirltacular over at the middle school.

"I don't know," I wailed. By this time, Mark and Kevin had come over, lured by the sound of my tears.

"Why is Allie crying?" Mark wanted to know.

"She doesn't have a present for Brittany's party," Uncle Jay explained.

"Oooh," Kevin said, looking concerned. "That's bad."

This just made me cry harder.

I really couldn't even remember anymore why I'd said

I'd go to this stupid party in the first place. Nothing was turning out the way I'd imagined. All my good friends were off having fun without me, and I was left with nothing but mean friends, who were going to kill me because I didn't have a present for the main mean girl.

"We have to go to the mall really quick," I said, doing my best to wipe my eyes with the sleeve of my purple shirt. "We have to buy Brittany a present that costs equal to or more than whatever her parents are spending on what I'll be eating at her party, my photo at Glitterati, and the cost of my share of the room at the Hilton Hotel."

"That's ridiculous," Uncle Jay said. "First of all, we don't have time to go to the mall, because your ride is coming any minute. And second of all, I don't have any money."

"How can you not have any money?" I asked him. "You just said Mom and Dad left you a hundred dollars!"

"That's for us to eat with while they're gone!" Uncle Jay cried. "I'm not blowing it all on a present for some girl who used to call you Allie Stinkle."

Mark started laughing. "Allie Stinkle! That's a good one."

"Shut up, *Mark* Stinkle," I said to him. "Don't you have any money of your own?" I asked Uncle Jay. "You have a job at Pizza Express!"

"I'm not spending my hard-earned money on a birthday present for Brittany Hauser," Uncle Jay declared, "a girl you don't even like. And that thing about how the present has to cost a certain amount — that's just insane. A present should come from the heart. And so should an invitation. Why did this girl even invite you to her party if she calls you names?"

"Because," I said, "I think her mom is impressed that our mom is the star of a TV show. Even though Mom doesn't get paid for being on *Good News!* But Brittany's mom doesn't know that."

Uncle Jay made a face. "And why do you want to go to this party again?"

I didn't want to have to bring up the limo and Glitterati and The Cheesecake Factory and the hotel thing. I just pressed my lips together and glared at him.

Finally, Uncle Jay said, "If you're so concerned about bringing a gift to this party, go upstairs to your room and find something in it that you think this girl would like and bring it down here and I'll wrap it for you."

My mouth dropped open. "I can't give Brittany Hauser a *used* gift!"

Mark, who is a boy and doesn't know anything about girl stuff, started laughing at this idea. Even Kevin, who is only *six*, looked appalled.

But Uncle Jay defended himself.

"For Pete's sake, Allie, you have a million books in your room. Give her a book. Books make the best gifts because you can open them again and again. Pick out your favorite book and tell her you wanted to share it with her because it meant so much to you. That's what I always give my friends on their birthdays — the gift of my favorite book. Now go do it, quick, before she gets here."

I thought about what Uncle Jay had said. The gift of a book was a good idea.

And I did have a lot of books. Some of them even looked new because I like to keep my books in very good condition.

And Brittany could stand to learn a little. Maybe if she read more books, she wouldn't do things like put her mother's cat in a suitcase (although I doubted she'd ever do that again, after her punishment last time).

"It's here!" Kevin suddenly yelled. "The limo!"

We all ran to look out the window. It was true. A huge white SUV limo, almost as long as our front yard, had pulled up outside. You could hear rock music blaring from it. Twinkly purple lights were flashing all around the bottom of it.

"Go get a book!" Uncle Jay yelled at me. "I'll stall them."

I ran up the stairs faster than I've ever run up them before. I burst into my room, startling Mewsie, who'd been grooming himself on my bed. He arched his back and hissed, then realized it was me and calmed down.

Panting, I scanned my bookshelf. What to give Brittany Hauser? A copy of one of the Boxcar Children? No, she would think that was too babyish.

Nancy Drew? She would think it was too old-fashioned.

The Narnia chronicles? I wasn't sure Brittany would believe you could stumble through a wardrobe and find a magical world.

Harry Potter? Brittany had probably seen all the movies and would think she wouldn't have to read the books.

So what?

Outside, I could hear my brother Kevin's voice. He was demanding a tour of the inside of the limo. Ordinarily, I would be mortified by this, but in this case I was proud of him. He was trying to buy me time to make my selection . . .

. . . while at the same time achieving his own dream of getting to sit inside a limo.

I was *very* proud of him.

Finally, my gaze landed on the perfect book. Of course. Why hadn't I thought of it before? And I had two copies, one in perfect condition because Harmony had given it to me, not knowing I'd already read it a million times. It had been her favorite growing up, too.

I didn't really want to give it to Brittany, even if I did have two copies of it. I mean, it was my favorite book.

And the copy from Harmony was so clean and nice. And inside the front cover, she'd written, *To a true friend.* It didn't have my name, or her name, or anything. So you couldn't tell who it was to or from. I could still give it to Brittany.

Even though she wasn't my true friend.

On the other hand, I didn't have much of a choice. It was this or nothing.

I grabbed the book and ran downstairs.

"Here," I said, practically throwing it at Uncle Jay.

He looked down at what he held.

"Good choice," he said, and went over to the dining room to begin wrapping it in that day's comic section from the newspaper. Really. The funny pages!

When I groaned, he looked at me. "What?" he said. "It's recycling. Very environmentally correct of you."

When he was done, he handed me the book and said, "Have a good time."

"I will." I was beginning to feel excited about going to the party again, now that I had a present and had actually seen the limo.

Uncle Jay was right. It didn't matter how expensive your gift was.

What mattered was that it came from the heart.

I grabbed my overnight bag, kissed Uncle Jay good-bye, and hurried outside. I was, I decided, going to have the time of my life.

RULE #7

Boy-crazy Girls Don't Understand That Not All Boys Are Great

"Your little brother," Brittany Hauser said when I'd finally pried Kevin out of the limo and climbed in myself and shut the door, "is kind of cute."

There was a general chime of agreement.

This, I knew, was a very good omen. Most people (who don't actually have to live with him) think my little brother Kevin is very cute. I could almost, in fact, forgive Kevin for the horrible thing that he had done, blabbing my secret to Marianne's little sister, since he had come out and won over the girls in this limo for me.

It wasn't the easiest audience, either, since it included not only Brittany Hauser, the ringleader of the "Allie Stinkle" episode, but also Mary Kay Shiner, my ex-best friend, who'd once told the whole school that I kept a book of rules (which I don't think is weird at all. What I think is weird is people who *don't* keep a book of rules. How can you know how to act if you don't know what the rules are?).

"Ha, thanks," I said.

I'll admit, I was a little nervous. The chauffeur (the limo was driven by a chauffeur! He had a uniform and a special hat and everything!) had come around when I'd dragged my suitcase up to the limo and put it in the trunk, then held the door open for me. Like I was a movie star or something! No one had ever done this for me before.

And then, when I got into the limo, I'd found five pairs of eyes staring at me — not counting Mrs. Hauser's, because she was sitting in the front seat with the driver.

There was Brittany, of course, the birthday girl. And Courtney Wilcox, Brittany's ex-best friend, who'd been replaced by *my* ex-best friend, Mary Kay Shiner, who was sitting on the other side of Brittany.

And there were two other girls I remembered from our class in Walnut Knolls Elementary: Lauren Freeman and Paige Moseley.

All the girls were dressed super stylishly, with lip gloss and little purses and — I should have known — high-heeled zip-up boots.

I looked sadly down at my cowboy boots. Sometimes it feels like no matter how hard I try, I can never win. This should be a rule.

"Hi, Allie," Mrs. Hauser called from the front of the car. It was like she was a million miles away. Seriously, that's how long the limo was. The seats in the back were so long, we could all have lain down on them and had room to spare. "It's lovely to see you."

"Hi, Mrs. Hauser," I called to her. "Thank you very much for having me."

My mom told me that *Thank you very much for having me* is what you say when someone invites you to a birthday party. It's a rule.

"You're so welcome," Mrs. Hauser said. "I understand that your parents are out of town?"

"Yes, ma'am," I said. Saying *yes, ma'am* and *no, sir* are other things my mom and dad told us we have to say to grown-ups when we're invited somewhere. That's another rule.

"Well, I hope you're having fun with your babysitter," Mrs. Hauser said.

"We don't have a babysitter," I said. "It's just my uncle Jay. It was going to be my great-aunt Joyce, but she threw her back out washing her cat."

"Oh, dear," Mrs. Hauser said. She knew all about washing cats, having a show cat of her own, Mewsie's mom, Lady Serena Archibald. "I hope she'll be all right. And please let your mom know when she gets home how much I enjoyed her review of *The Mirror Is Myself*."

"Oh, I will," I said. Even though I knew my mom had hated that movie.

"How's Mewsie?" Mrs. Hauser wanted to know.

"Mewsie's fine!" I said. I was so glad Mrs. Hauser had asked. Since her cat, Lady Serena Archibald, was Mewsie's mom, that made Mrs. Hauser Mewsie's grandma. "He's so cute! The other day, he was chasing his tail, and —"

"That's enough questions, Mom!" Brittany said, and pulled on my arm so that I sank down on one of the long seats next to her and Mary Kay, and opposite Courtney, Lauren, and Paige.

"She talks so much," Brittany said, about her mom. Loud enough for her to hear, too! "It's so annoying!"

Just then, though, the car started up. So maybe Mrs. Hauser didn't hear how rude her daughter was being. I took the opportunity to look around.

Sad as I was about how I hadn't gone with Erica and those guys and how I'd worn all the wrong things, I still couldn't believe it. I was finally in a limo!

It was even better than I'd thought it would be. First of all, there was a TV in it, right in the back of Mrs. Hauser's seat. It was on, and it was playing Hannah Montana's concert movie (only the sound was turned way down).

Second of all, there were blinking lights everywhere. The whole inside of the car was bathed in purple. There was a bar — a real bar! — with every kind of soda you could think of to drink, with real glasses that tinkled as the car drove along, and a little refrigerator with a glass door. The inside was all lit up so you could see what kind of snacks they had, like Snickers and M&Ms and potato chips and little jars of nuts.

Weirdest of all, the roof over our heads was nothing but twinkling little stars going on and off in all different spots, like airplane lights, only they made shapes, like the constellations . . . except instead of rotating around the earth slowly, the way the constellations do, they were going by at, like, a thousand miles an hour, all over the roof of the limo.

Brittany must have noticed me admiring this, since she said, "Your little brother was really interested in the moon roof, too. I let him work the controls. It goes at different speeds. The buttons are right here, see?"

She showed me the console, which was right behind where she was sitting. I was probably as excited to push the buttons as Kevin had been, but I tried to control myself, since I am a fourth-grader, not a kindergartner.

Still, it was so cool! One button made the twinkling stars on the roof change speed in their twinkling, and another changed their color. Another one changed the color of the lights on the inside of the car. They turned from purple to pink, then pink to gold, then white, then blue, then red.

"We thought purple was prettiest," Paige told me in a friendly way. It was clear they'd been playing with the buttons the whole way across town to pick me up.

"Check out this one," Brittany said, and pushed another button. A screen went up between our seats and the front seat where her mom and the driver sat.

"See ya, Mom!" Brittany yelled, and she and Mary Kay started cackling.

"Oh, Brittany," Mrs. Hauser said, rolling her eyes just as the screen went all the way up and she vanished from view.

"Good riddance," Brittany said, like she was glad to be rid of her mom. Which I thought was kind of mean, since she hadn't actually been bothering us, as far as I could tell.

Brittany pushed another button, and the sound to the Hannah Montana concert movie turned way up. Then she pushed another, and the lights around us all started going crazy, like they do at the skating rink when it's couples-only skate.

Then Brittany turned to me and said, "Caramel corn?" She had a whole bag she'd taken from the mini refrigerator. I could tell, because it was the same size as the empty space in the fridge.

"Thanks," I said, and took a big handful. It was delicious.

"So," Brittany said, as I was chewing. "Do you have a boyfriend?"

I nearly choked on my popcorn, I so wasn't expecting this question.

"Uh." I looked around at the other girls. They were all staring at me super intently, waiting for my answer. Mary Kay, who usually started crying at the drop of a hat, showed no sign of doing so now, to my surprise.

I wasn't sure what the right answer was. I mean, at Pine Heights, fourth-graders aren't allowed to have boyfriends and girlfriends, by order of Mrs. Hunter and Mrs. Danielson, the fourth-grade teachers. I hadn't heard about any fifth-graders going with each other, either. It simply wasn't stylish at Pine Heights for people — with the exception of Cheyenne O'Malley — to do that. It just wasn't that kind of school.

When I'd left it, Walnut Knolls hadn't been, either.

But who knows what had happened since I'd left? Maybe it had become a total boyfriend-girlfriend kind of school. Maybe Brittany was going with Scott Stamphley now.

It was weird, but the idea of Brittany going with Scott Stamphley sort of made me want to throw up the caramel corn I was eating.

It also made me not want to give her the book I'd picked out so especially for her anymore.

I really didn't know how to answer her question. If I said I didn't have a boyfriend, was she going to say I was immature, like Cheyenne O'Malley always did? On the one hand, I didn't care. But on the other hand, twenty-four hours is a long time to have to put up with someone. I didn't want to start off my visit with Brittany on the wrong foot.

Then, when I really thought about it, I realized that, technically, I'd *almost* had a boyfriend. I mean, Joey Fields *had* wanted to go with me.

Even if Cheyenne O'Malley had talked him into it. And I'd said no because he is basically the weirdest boy on the entire planet.

But there was no reason those girls had to know that.

"I guess I could have had a boyfriend," I said slowly. "If I'd wanted one. Because there was this kid who liked me. But I didn't want to go with him. Because I think fourth grade is too young to be tied down."

I had totally heard that line, about not wanting to be tied down, in a movie once.

Brittany and Mary Kay exchanged glances.

"See?" Brittany said to Mary Kay. "I told you. You owe me five dollars."

Finally, Mary Kay looked like the old Mary Kay I knew so well. Her eyes filled up with tears.

"It's not fair," Mary Kay said, digging around in her purse. "Everyone's got a boy who wants to go with them but *me!*"

"My mom said that your mom said a boy wanted to go with you," Brittany informed me smugly. "But Mary Kay didn't believe me."

I didn't care about this. I needed to find out which boy wanted to go with Brittany. Suddenly, it was super important to me.

"Oh?" I asked casually. "So people are going with each other at Walnut Knolls?"

Lauren and Paige and Brittany all screamed. I noticed Courtney didn't scream. Courtney was just sitting there, playing with her necklace. Mary Kay was, as usual, trying not to cry.

"No!" Lauren explained, laughing. "No one goes with anybody at Walnut Knolls. All the boys there are so immature!"

Suddenly, I felt much, much better. I didn't even mind the crazily blinking lights anymore. I dug my hand into the bag Brittany held for more popcorn.

"Last weekend we went to Lauren's cousin Jake's bar mitzvah," Brittany explained, "and there were some cute boys from the middle school there."

"One of them even asked Brittany to dance," Paige said teasingly as Brittany blushed. Really! I'd never seen Brittany blush before . . .

. . . although it only became obvious that's what she was doing when the lights in the limo went white.

"He was just a sixth-grader," Brittany said.

"And he didn't know you were a fourth-grader," Mary Kay pointed out, not very nicely.

"Shut up," Brittany said, also not very nicely.

It was kind of weird being around these girls. They were a little mean to each other. Not like Erica and Caroline and Sophie, who were more supportive of one another. Even Rosemary, who wasn't interested in things like boyfriends and dances, would have had friendlier things to say than these girls.

"I can't believe a boy asked you to go with him," Brittany said, looking at me — *me!* — admiringly, "and you turned him down, Allie."

If Brittany had had the slightest idea who the boy was — that he usually barked instead of talked, and that I had to sit next to him all day long, and that he stole all of Mrs.

Hunter's Boxcar Children books and generally drove me crazy — she would not be saying this.

But *boy-crazy girls don't understand that not all boys are great.* That's a rule.

"Yeah, well," I said, trying to look casual and sophisticated. I was in a limo, after all, eating caramel corn, so this wasn't hard. "When you're around boys as much as I am, you kind of get used to it. At my new school, my teacher put me in charge of the boys." This wasn't technically a lie, either. Rosemary and I are in charge of all the boys in the last row of Room 209. "Because of my little brothers, she thinks I kind of have a way with them."

"You are so lucky," Paige breathed. "I wish I could change schools and get to sit with boys!"

"Are they cute?" Lauren wanted to know.

Cute? Joey Fields, who had only recently started remembering to wash his face and comb his hair in the morning before school? Patrick Day, who liked to pick his nose (and yes, possibly even eat it)? Stuart Maxwell, who tried daily to draw the most disgusting pictures of zombies that he could, and thus gross me out?

"Totally cute," I lied.

"Lucky!" all the girls cried in unison.

The thing was, they were never going to find out that the boys in Room 209 *totally* weren't cute. So who even cared? And the things I was saying weren't *total* lies. If you didn't know them, Joey, Patrick, and Stuart might *seem* cute . . .

. . . the same way that boy at Lauren's cousin's bar mitzvah had thought Brittany *seemed* older than a fourth-grader.

And the other thing was, if you didn't know Brittany, you might think she *seemed* nice, too.

Except that I knew she totally wasn't.

Another person I got the feeling knew she totally wasn't was Courtney Wilcox.

Oh, Courtney had come to Brittany's party and all.

But it didn't seem like she was super friendly with Brittany or with any of her other friends. She laughed in all the right places, and she joined us in raiding the limo's fridge.

But she didn't seem to have that much to say. Mostly, she just sat there and played with her necklace and stared at the blinking lights.

Brittany acted nice to me, though, all the way to the Glitterati store in the city. It was amazing. She treated me as if we'd always been best friends, and the thing with Lady Serena Archibald and my shoving a cupcake in her face had never happened. Even Mary Kay acted nice to me — not quite as nice as Brittany, though, since I don't think Mary Kay had quite gotten over the fact that she and I had once been best friends and used to play lions and ride bikes together, and now we hadn't spoken in months, thanks to her telling everyone about my book of rules . . .

. . . which everyone was politely avoiding mentioning.

Even Lauren and Paige were nice to me, I guess because they were impressed by all the tips I gave them about boys (like, for instance, that boys like it when you tell them what to do, especially when you do it in a strong, firm voice, the way you'd address your kitten when he's done something wrong. Which is really true. At least for the boys in the last row of Room 209. Oh, sure, they *act* like they don't like it. But they always end up doing what Rosemary and I say in the end. Like, when we go, "Stop kicking our chairs!"

they always do. Especially when we add, "Or we'll tell Mrs. Hunter!").

It was like the girls in that limo had never been around a boy before in their lives. That's how ignorant they were of how to act around them. I swear. I could have told them, "And boys really like it if you put a clown mask on your head and strap a kangaroo tail around your waist and then hop around like an idiot."

They totally would have believed me.

By the time the limo pulled up to Glitterati, I was a little hoarse from talking so much. Plus, my stomach was a little queasy from all the soda and candy I'd eaten from the mini fridge. And the blinking lights had kind of given me a headache.

So I was really relieved when Mr. Fernando — that was our driver — opened the door and said, "Ladies? You've arrived at your destination," and a big rush of cool air came into the car.

And there, before us, was Glitterati.

RULE #8

You Can't Do Something to Make the Birthday Girl Unhappy on Purpose on Her Birthday

Glitterati was just the way it had looked in all the pictures I'd seen. It was huge and sparkly and filled with loud, up-tempo music that seemed to fill my whole body and drum against the inside of my chest in a happy, boppy beat.

It was exactly what I'd hoped it would be, and more.

I was so excited I thought I was going to explode.

And not just from all the Coke and M&Ms I'd had in the limo.

"Hi, I'm Summer," yelled the pretty girl with the spiky hair who met us at the door (she had to yell to be heard over the music). "I'll be your Glitterati guide for the day.

I'm here to make sure your Glitterati experience is everything that it can be. I want to get you *pumped!*"

Summer didn't need to worry. I was already pumped. So was everybody else. Except maybe Mrs. Hauser. She looked like her head hurt a little from all the music.

"The first thing we need to do," Summer yelled, "is explain that Glitterati isn't just a store. It's a way of life. At Glitterati, we encourage kids to use their imaginations and creativity to envision their future and themselves exactly the way they've always wanted to, without limitations!"

When Summer said the word "limitations," she threw something at us. It turned out to be gold sparkles. It got all over us . . . our hair, our clothes . . . everywhere. Mrs. Hauser backed out of the way so it wouldn't get on her and the fur trim of her coat.

"There!" Summer yelled. "Now you've been Glitteratied!"

This was awesome. I had always wanted to be Glitteratied.

"Today, as long as you wear your Glitterati dust," Summer went on, "all your dreams will come true. If you've always wanted to be an undercover rock star, at Glitterati we can help make you an undercover rock star. If you've always wanted to be an urban fairy, like me, we can make that dream come true, too. Glitterati is about expressing your individuality while promoting a unique shopping experience that makes every kid feel special!"

Whoa. Maybe it was because I'd been Glitteratied, but I was ready to feel special. Also, unique.

I could tell Summer was unique because she had some sparkly star stickers right next to her eyes.

I wanted some sparkly star stickers next to my eyes, too. This, I felt sure, would make me be as special and unique as Summer.

"So," Summer yelled at us. "Are you ready?"

"Yes," we all yelled back. Even Mary Kay, who never yelled.

"Then let's go express our individuality!" Summer yelled.

We all ran screaming into the costume racks, where Summer said we could decide on what looks we wanted to use to express our individuality.

"I'm going to be an urban fairy, like Summer," Paige yelled. She was pawing through the fairy costumes, looking for one exactly like Summer's, which was tight jeans and a black sparkle halter top.

"No," Lauren said. "*I'm* going to be an urban fairy!"

"You guys." Mary Kay looked like she was about to burst into tears. "*I'm* going to be an urban fairy! We can't all be urban fairies. You have to be something else."

I couldn't believe it. They all wanted to be urban fairies.

And it was probably just because Summer had been dressed like one.

Which wasn't really all that unique or individual, if you thought about it.

It was true I'd wanted to get shooting star stickers next to my eyes like Summer. But I still wanted to dress as an actress slash veterinarian for my photo shoot.

I shook my head in disgust over the other girls, then went to the rack marked SUPERSTAR. There were lots of fake leather jackets and tight short skirts. Also, knee-high zip-up high-heeled boots. In just about every color you could imagine.

This was *exactly* what I would imagine an actress slash veterinarian would wear. You know, for doing her important acting and animal healing work. It was amazing, but the Glitterati dust was already working! It was helping me to envision my future career. Well, what I was going to wear while I was doing it, anyway.

"None of you can be urban fairies," Brittany yelled. "Because *I'm* going to be an urban fairy. And it's *my* birthday. I'll figure out something else for you to be."

Paige and Lauren looked super disappointed. Mary Kay started to cry. Courtney, who hadn't joined in with any of them, anyway, just rolled her eyes and shrugged.

I guess Summer could see some of Brittany's party guests were having trouble envisioning their futures and expressing their individuality (only not me. Because I had already picked out a purple zebra-striped fake leather jacket, a black mini sparkle skirt, red shirt, and black zip-up high-heeled boots), since she came up to us and went, "So, ladies. What have we decided?"

"Well, I'm going to be an urban fairy," Brittany said. "Since it's my birthday." Then she started pointing at each of us. "She," she said, pointing at Paige, "is going to be an undercover rock star, and she," pointing at Mary Kay, "is going to be a prep school princess. And she," pointing at Lauren, "is going to be a teen superstar, and she," pointing to Courtney, "is going to be a teen goth vampire, and she," pointing at me, "is going to be a pirate."

"Sounds good," Summer said. "Let's get to the makeover booths for our transformations!"

"Wait a minute." I couldn't believe what I'd just heard. "A *pirate*? I'm not going to be a pirate."

"Sure you are," Brittany said. "You love pirates. Everyone loves pirates."

"I do not love pirates," I said. "My little brother Kevin loves pirates. But he's six."

"You have to be a pirate," Brittany said. "Everybody else has taken all the other costumes."

"No, they haven't." I showed her the clothes I was holding. "I want to be an actress slash veterinarian. No one else is dressing up as an actress slash veterinarian."

"Whoever heard of an actress slash veterinarian?" Brittany asked, bewildered.

"Me," I said. "I have. It's what I want to be when I grow up. An actress who is also a veterinarian who saves the lives of baby animals."

"You can't be an actress *and* a veterinarian," Brittany said. "You can be one thing or the other, but you can't be both."

"Yes, you can," I said. "I've been Glitteratied. I can be anything I want to be. Summer said so."

"I think since this Glitterati Girl already has her look pulled together," Summer said, pointing to all the clothes in my arms, "we might as well let her head to the makeover booths for her transformation. Maybe another one of your friends wants to be a pirate, Brittany."

Brittany shook her head, staring at me. I didn't know when I'd done it, but I could tell by the look on her face that I'd somehow wandered over to Brittany's bad side.

See, this was exactly why I had the book of rules. Because you could never tell when you were going to do something to make a girl mad at you . . . without even meaning to! All I'd done was say I didn't want to be a pirate.

And now the birthday girl was mad at me.

"No," Brittany said, narrowing her eyes at me. "Allie wants to be a pirate. Don't you, Allie?"

I absolutely did not want to be a pirate. I did not want to dress like one or have my photo taken as one. I never, ever, not once in my life had expressed a single desire to be or look like a pirate. This was not the vision I had for my future. I wanted to be an actress slash veterinarian. I had my costume all ready to go.

But I could tell by the look on Brittany's face that if I didn't do what she said, I was going to be in big trouble. Just like the time when Brittany had put Lady Serena Archibald in the suitcase.

And like that time, I didn't want to back down. I didn't want to give up on my dream of being an actress slash veterinarian.

But this wasn't like someone putting a live animal into a suitcase. This was just a girl who wanted me to dress a certain way and get my picture taken. Also, it was her birthday. Not mine.

You can't do something to make the birthday girl unhappy on purpose on her birthday.

That was a rule.

And one I'd learned the hard way, way back on Mary Kay's birthday. It was one of the reasons why Mary Kay and I weren't best friends anymore.

I had ended up realizing Mary Kay hadn't been the world's best friend, anyway.

But I didn't want to ruin Brittany's birthday the way I had Mary Kay's, either. This wasn't a good way to make — or keep — friends.

And the truth was, what did it matter? It was one day.

And just because I dressed like a pirate while wearing Glitterati dust didn't mean I was going to magically transform into a pirate when I grew up.

That's a rule.

"Fine," I said, and handed my pile of stuff to Lauren. She was the one who was getting to be a teen superstar, after all. "I'll be a pirate."

And that's exactly what I ended up being. I couldn't believe it. I let Summer pick out a girl pirate outfit for me — stupid baggy boots, black velvet pants, white blouse, red sash, sword, vest, basically what my brother Kevin had insisted on wearing to school every day for months — then headed over to the makeover booths for my transformation, where a guy about Uncle Jay's age, only his name was Randy, ran a straight iron through my hair and put some eyeliner on me that he said was the same kind Keira Knightley wore in the Pirates of the Caribbean movies.

But when I finally saw my reflection in the big dressing room mirror, I didn't look very different from when I'd sat down a few minutes before.

So I asked Randy if I could please have some sparkle stickers on my face like Summer's.

He said yes, and put one on the corner of my right eye.

Only since I was dressed like a pirate, not a fairy, mine was a single diamond teardrop . . .

. . . to represent my deep well of sorrow for my victims, Randy said.

So that, at least, was okay.

Then it was time to see how everyone else's transformations had turned out.

I came out of my makeover booth waving my sword, feeling

a little better about not getting to be an actress slash veterinarian. Because I actually looked like a pretty cool pirate lady.

But when they saw me, Brittany, Lauren, Paige, and Mary Kay started laughing.

"Oh, no," Brittany said. "Allie, you look so stupid."

"Why?" I looked down at myself. "I'm a pirate. This is how you told me to dress."

"I know," Brittany said, still laughing. "But I didn't know it would be so dumb."

"Brittany!" Mrs. Hauser was there, taking pictures of all of us. "Allie, you look adorable. You don't look dumb at all."

But actually, compared to the other girls, I did look dumb. They seemed super grown-up and sophisticated in their outfits as superstars, rock stars, prep school princesses, goth vampires, and urban fairies. I was the only one who looked like a kid wearing a Halloween costume. Even with my diamond teardrop of sorrow.

"I told you," I said, fingering my red sash. "Pirates are for six-year-olds."

"I thought you'd be a cool pirate," Brittany said. "Like Keira Knightley. But I guess not. Oh, well."

That's all. Just *Oh, well.* Like it didn't matter that she'd destroyed my unique shopping experience at Glitterati. Which I guess I wasn't really having, anyway, since I didn't have any money so I couldn't really buy anything. But still. What about my chance to exercise my imagination and creativity and live my dream of envisioning my future and all of that? Unlike my little brother, I had never envisioned my future as a *pirate*, for Pete's sake.

"You all look *amazing!*" the photographer, Dusty, cried. Dusty had an earring in one ear, like Randy, and long hair. He also wore a lot of necklaces. "Come on, let's work the runway now, shall we? Shall we? Who's going first? Birthday girl?"

"No," Brittany said. "Paige. You go."

Paige swept back some of her flat-ironed, rock-star hair. "Cool," she said, and climbed up onto the runway. As the music thumped overhead, she walked down the red carpet, while Dusty said, "Great! Fantastic! You're a rock star! You're amazing!"

"Thank you," Paige said, politely, when she reached the end of the stage. Then she jumped down.

If you asked me, the whole thing was quite a letdown. I mean, Paige didn't really *work the runway* like the models on those shows Harmony likes to watch when she comes over and my mom and dad aren't home. I mean, she just walked down the runway. She didn't *sashay*, or *work it, girl*, or try to be *fierce*, or *smile with her eyes*.

As soon as Paige left the runway, Brittany interrogated her, which means asked her a lot of questions.

"How was it?" Brittany asked her, about the runway.

"Nice," Paige said with a shrug.

"Not weird?" Brittany asked her. The runway was at the center of the store, so everyone could see you when you came down it. I guess that's what Brittany meant. She was worried about people looking at her.

"No," Paige said. "I mean, it's kind of scary. But I just tried to go down it as fast as I could."

"Good," Brittany said. "Lauren, you go next."

So Lauren did. Basically, the same thing happened to her. Summer and Mrs. Hauser and the rest of us sat in the audience, cheering for her, while Dusty took pictures. But, like Paige, Lauren didn't do anything interesting on the runway. She basically ran down it, pausing only to let Dusty take her picture.

The same thing happened with Mary Kay, Courtney, and Brittany. Finally, it was my turn.

When it was my turn on the runway, I decided I was going to do something different from the other girls. I tried to envision my future — what it was going to be like when I was a world-famous actress slash veterinarian, and I'd be walking down red carpets, getting my picture taken all the time. I was going to have to get used to it, because this was what my life was going to be like . . . riding in limos, strolling down runways, having the paparazzi snap my photo all over the place, with huge crowds begging for my autograph. My life wouldn't really be my own anymore. Everyone was going to want a piece of me, because I'd be so famous for being in so many movies and saving so many people's pets.

As I came down the runway — to the song "I'm Gonna Knock You Out," which I thought was kind of ironic, because that was the same song Missy was doing her routine to, and I couldn't help wondering how her performance was going, and how much better a time Erica, Caroline, and Sophie were having than I was (I bet they were having a way better time than I was) — I tried to do what I thought was a really good runway walk, the kind I saw the models doing on TV. I also tried to make sure to smile at everyone in the store as I went past them. Missy, I knew, would be smiling at all the judges as she did her twirling. None of the other girls at Brittany's party had smiled as they'd run-walked down the runway.

But Missy had told us that making good eye contact with your audience, especially the judges, is way important if you want to score perfect tens.

And even though no one at Glitterati was judging me, I still wanted perfect tens. I mean, why not try your hardest, all the time, even if you're just in some dumb store at a birthday party instead of at the Little Miss Majorette Baton Twirling Twirltacular, middle school division?

It's all good practice for later, when it really counts, right? That's a rule.

As I went down the runway at Glitterati, I pretended that all the other customers in the store were autograph seekers who loved my latest film — or pet owners whose dogs I'd saved. I really turned on the charm. I wasn't dressed the way I wanted to be — Brittany had seen to that.

But that didn't mean I couldn't use my imagination and creativity, the way Summer had suggested — to make the best of the situation. That was what acting was all about, right?

When I got to the end of the runway — where Dusty was going, "You're amazing, Allie! That's fantastic! You're really bringing it, darlin'!" — and I was sure I had the attention of everyone in the store, I got an idea. It was kind of silly, but I thought, *Why not? You're only in Glitterati once.*

So just as the music went, "I'm . . . gonna knock *you* out!" I pulled my pirate sword from my red sash, bared my teeth, and lunged at Dusty with the tip of my sword, yelling, "Aaaaargh!" the way a lady pirate would, right on time with the word "out."

I stopped only when the tip of my blade was just a couple of inches from his camera lens. This was also when Missy finished her routine, standing with her baton raised and her back arched.

There was a moment of surprised silence following my doing this (except for the pulsing rock music from the store's speakers, of course).

Uh-oh, I thought. Had I gone too far? Mrs. Hauser and the girls in the audience looked completely shocked for a few seconds, like I had tried to bite Dusty, not given him a pirate *Argh!*

Did they not know the first thing about pirates? I mean, everyone knows pirates say *Argh!* and try to stab people. It was a *joke*. Didn't they get it? I'd been trying to be funny!

Then, as I held the pose, feeling tiny beads of sweat breaking out beneath my hair as the lights from above the runway shined down on me, thinking, *Dusty, take the picture. Take the picture already, Dusty,* Dusty started to laugh.

"Beautiful!" he cried. "Perfect! That's the best shot of the day, Allie. That one will go up in our Hall of Fame, for sure."

And he snapped the picture.

Around the store, a few of the customers started to applaud. Some of them just shook their heads, but others laughed. I straightened up and bowed, the way Mrs. Hunter had shown us.

I'd done it! I'd made everyone in Glitterati laugh! Well, almost everyone.

It felt great, as always.

"Thanks," I said. I was a bit sweaty beneath my newly straight-ironed hair. But I didn't care. "No applause, please, just throw money. Kidding, I'm kidding."

I jumped off the runway and came over to the other girls. They were all smiling.

Well, all except Brittany and Mary Kay.

Oops.

"Oh, Allie," Mrs. Hauser cried, putting her arm around me. "That was hilarious! You're such a performer! I think you're going to follow in your mother's footsteps and have your own TV show."

"Thanks," I said, still panting a little. It was hot in that pirate costume. "I guess I am."

"You were so funny," Lauren said, punching me in the arm. But not hard. "Argh!"

"Argh!" Paige said, laughing. "Like Jack Sparrow!"

"That was really good," Courtney said, still fiddling with the necklace she wore beneath her plastic goth vampire outfit. "All those people were looking, and you didn't even seem to care or be embarrassed."

Brittany and Mary Kay both looked as if they cared that everyone in the store had been looking. They looked as if they cared a lot.

But that wasn't my fault! Brittany was the one who'd made me wear the pirate outfit in the first place. If she hadn't wanted me to act like a pirate, she shouldn't have picked this costume for me. I was just following Summer's instructions, making my Glitterati experience be all it could be.

"Okay," Dusty said, coming over. "Here we go. Your Glitterati memory cards, so you can always treasure your trip to Glitterati and share it with your friends and loved ones."

He had the photos from our trips down the runway! He handed each of us a big photo of ourselves in our chosen costume. Each one was set in a purple folding cardboard frame, encrusted with glitter.

I probably don't have to point out that each girl looked amazingly glamorous in her picture. You could barely recognize Mary Kay, for instance, in her prep school princess boarding school uniform, with her hair ironed so straight and held back in a black velvet band. Or Brittany as an urban fairy, in her halter top and tight jeans.

But the one that was especially hilarious was mine, lunging at the camera and making a face just like a pirate. I started laughing just like everyone else when I saw it. It wasn't the same as the other girls' more glamorous shots.

But Kevin, I knew, would love it. If I had to play a pirate, at least I'd played the part the way a real actress would have. I couldn't wait to show my photo to Erica, Sophie, and Caroline.

Then I remembered, with a pang, that I was probably never going to get to show my Glitterati card to those guys. Because it would be kind of rude of me to rub it in to them about how I'd gone to Glitterati today with Brittany, instead of to Missy's Twirltacular. "It would be fun and everything," Sophie had said of Glitterati. "But only if you went with your real friends."

She had been so right! My Glitterati experience would have been completely different if I'd gone there with Erica, Sophie, and Caroline (and even Rosemary, though I couldn't imagine she'd have liked it that much). How I wished I had!

I wondered what all of them were doing right now, and how Missy was doing at her events. Was she going to bring home a trophy?

And I wished — more than I had ever wished anything — that I was at the middle school with my real friends instead of at Brittany's stupid birthday party. I had made a terrible choice.

And I was going to have to pay for it for the rest of my life, probably.

RULE #9

It's Important Always to Thank Your Hostess When You've Had a Nice Time . . . and Even When You Haven't

"Thank you," I said to Mrs. Hauser, after we'd changed back into our normal clothes and were headed toward the limo, waiting for us right in front of Glitterati, with Mr. Fernando, the driver, holding the door open for us — just like the coachman in *Cinderella*! "That was really fun."

It's important always to thank your hostess when you've had a nice time . . . and even when you haven't. That's a rule.

"Why, you're welcome, Allie," Mrs. Hauser said. "I'm sure you all must be as anxious to get to The Cheesecake

Factory as I am. All that modeling must have made you hungry!"

We all said we were.

But after Mr. Fernando closed the door behind us and started driving toward the restaurant, I found out that not everyone was looking forward to the meal. I mean, I knew I wasn't, because all I wanted to do was go home. And I still had dinner and the whole sleepover at the luxury hotel to get through.

But it turned out Brittany wasn't having a good time, either.

"It's just," she said, "that this isn't going to be any fun if you're not going to take it seriously, Allie."

I stared at her from where I was sitting on the huge long limo seat.

"What?" I had no idea what she was talking about. "Take what seriously?"

"My birthday," Brittany said. She was staring back at me from *her* long bench seat, which was across from mine, her arms folded across her chest. "You're treating it like it's a big joke."

My mouth dropped open. "I am not!" I cried. "How can you even say that?"

How *could* she say that? I'd said thank you to her mother for paying for my Glitterati photo session and everything!

"That thing," Brittany said accusingly, "where you posed like a pirate on the runway and said *argh*. Everyone was looking!"

I glanced at Paige and Lauren, both of whom had laughed when I'd done that.

"It was a joke," I said. "Because I was dressed like a pirate. Everyone laughed. You guys laughed!"

They weren't laughing now, though.

"Brittany was embarrassed," Paige said.

"Yeah," Lauren said. "You shouldn't have embarrassed her."

I glared at them. "Well, how do you think *I* felt?" I asked. "When Brittany made me dress up like a pirate, which is something my six-year-old brother dresses as, by the way."

"You looked cute," Brittany said.

"You said I looked dumb," I reminded her.

"No, I didn't," Brittany said. "I said you looked cute."

"No, you didn't," I said. "You said I looked dumb."

Brittany glanced at her friends. "I would never say something like that," she said. "Would I, you guys?"

All of them shook their heads. Except Courtney, who'd taken out her cell phone and was texting someone. Or pretending like she was, anyway. Clearly, Courtney did not want to get involved.

"Allie," Mary Kay said, "it's really mean of you to say Brittany would say something like that. Just because you're, like, the most popular girl in your new school and you never even call us anymore and your mom is a big TV star and you have a boyfriend —"

"I do not have a boyfriend," I said. I couldn't believe this. "I told you! I said I wouldn't go with him! And my mom doesn't even get paid for being on TV!"

"Oh, right," Brittany said, rolling her eyes. "You expect us to believe that?"

"It's true!" I cried.

How could this be happening? I knew I wasn't Brittany's

favorite person. But I hadn't expected to be outright attacked at her birthday party, for things that weren't my fault, or that I hadn't done on purpose. Why would she even have invited me to her party if it was just to pick on me?

"I guess you think you're too good for us," Brittany said, "don't you, Allie, now that you go to your fancy new school, in your fancy new neighborhood with all those big houses, and have all your fancy new friends."

What was she even talking about? Had she seen my school? It was the oldest building in town, practically. It still had BOYS written over one door and GIRLS written over the other. And my house was just as old. And my friends weren't fancy! They were the sweetest girls in the world. They'd rather play games of let's pretend than get manicures! They liked to mattress surf.

In fact, I really wished I was with them right now, instead of with Brittany and her friends. I had made the biggest mistake ever coming to Brittany's party instead of the Little Miss Majorette Baton Twirling Twirltacular.

Thankfully, the limo pulled to a stop at that moment, and the screen between the front seat and backseat came down.

"We're here, girls," Mrs. Hauser called. "Cheesecake Factory!"

"Yay!" Brittany said, in a fake voice, like she hadn't just been verbally assaulting me.

Mr. Fernando came around and opened the door for us, and Brittany got out.

"Don't forget your presents for me," she called sweetly. "I'm opening them before cake!"

Stupid Brittany, I thought as I dug around in my backpack for her present. And her stupid birthday party. And stupid me for ever having been stupid enough to come to it. I guess I was learning a pretty good lesson. Only I didn't know what that lesson was. Don't ever accept a party invitation if it includes riding in a limo? Well, that wasn't going to bode well for my future, in which I planned on riding in limos all the time.

Inside The Cheesecake Factory, it was insane. I had never been to such a fancy, crazy place. The walls were painted bright orange, and the ceiling was a million feet high, and there were people everywhere — so many people that the hostess had to give them all giant beepers and make them wait outside (even though it was kind of chilly out). When their beeper went off, that meant their table was ready.

We didn't get a beeper, though. Our table was waiting for us, because Mrs. Hauser had made a reservation and also called ahead to let the restaurant know we were on our way. When the hostess led us to where we were sitting, I saw that it was in a little alcove slightly away from the other tables, and that someone had decorated it all nice for Brittany's birthday. There were white balloons and streamers everywhere, and there were presents already piled up by the seat at the head of the table . . . Brittany's seat.

"Look how adorable," Lauren said, taking pictures with her cell phone camera. The other girls who had cell phone cameras took pictures, too.

I didn't, because I don't have a cell phone. My parents refuse to get me one, because my parents still live in the Stone Age, when fire hasn't been invented yet. Or the Internet.

Brittany looked absolutely delighted about her table full of presents. She went and took her place at the head of the table, in front of all her gifts.

This was the cue, I guess, for Mrs. Hauser to take her pictures. And for us to put down our presents. Each of the other girls had daintily wrapped gifts in pink and white wrapping paper with giant white bows. Mine, in its funny-pages wrapping, looked completely out of place in the pile.

"It's recycled paper," I joked as I set mine down, trying to make the most out of a situation that was so rapidly coming apart, it was like one of those paper towel commercials they show on TV, where they run water over the paper towel holding the brick until the paper towel shreds into a million pieces. "Environmentally correct!"

To my relief, everyone laughed. They were in a better mood now because a waitress had come by with giant glasses of pink lemonade for all of us, and a fancy drink with an umbrella in it for Mrs. Hauser.

"To the birthday girl," Mrs. Hauser said, and everyone held up their glass and toasted Brittany.

Brittany giggled and took a sip of her lemonade. Then the waitress started taking everyone's orders for dinner. I chose a cheeseburger and fries, with no tomato.

"Not even on the side," I said, because sometimes they try to put the tomato on the side. But I don't like it when they do that, because the little tomato seeds get all over the lettuce for the burger, and it's truly disgusting.

"No problem," the waitress said. "No tomato at all."

"Or ketchup," I said. "I don't like anything red on my plate. I'd like my burger well done, please, so there's no red in it."

"No red," the waitress said. "Got it."

I thought I heard Brittany, Mary Kay, Lauren, and Paige titter and whisper about this, but I didn't care. They should try having a food they hate show up on *their* plates all the time.

Brittany ordered a burger, too. She said, "I'll take mine with a tomato. You can put Allie's tomato on my plate. I don't mind. I'm not a freak about red food."

All the girls laughed, except Courtney and Mrs. Hauser, who said, "Now, Brittany, everyone has their likes and dislikes. You know how you are about cauliflower."

"Oh, Mother," Brittany said in disgust. "Everyone hates cauliflower. But who hates ketchup?"

Everyone turned to look at me. It's true, I am a bit of a freak. I just don't like to eat red things. They make the inside of my mouth feel itchy, and if I swallow them, they make me feel like I'm going to gag.

"Well," Mrs. Hauser said, "Allie is an original, and that's what makes her so fun."

She turned to her menu to see what she wanted to get, since it was her turn to order.

Yeah! That's right! I'm an original! I'm not like everybody else. Why would I want to be? I'm unique, a unique individual, like Summer at Glitterati! I was still wearing my sparkle teardrop, too, even though all the other girls had taken their stars off.

But I was still feeling a deep well of sorrow for all my pirate victims.

And for Brittany as well. Because I was never going to start liking her. Never, ever.

After the waitress went away, Brittany started opening her gifts. She had to, because if she didn't, there wouldn't be room for the food when they started bringing it out.

Brittany opened the biggest box in front of her first.

That was a present from her mom and dad. It turned out to be an iPod and a docking station with surround-sound speakers and a radio for her room, all in purple, Brittany's favorite color.

"Cool!" Brittany said. "Just what I wanted! Thanks, Mom."

I had always wanted one of those, too. But no one had gotten me that for my last birthday. I had just gotten a regular CD player. Which was nice, but you can't hook it up to a computer and download songs.

Brittany went to open her next present, which was from Mary Kay. It turned out to be an iTunes gift certificate, to go with her iPod.

"Wow!" Brittany said. "Thanks, Mary Kay!"

She and Mary Kay hugged. Mary Kay cried, as usual. But this time it was because she was so happy to be a part of Brittany's totally amazing birthday party.

I wished I had a spatula to stick down Mary Kay's throat.

But that was wrong of me, so I settled for sucking lemonade up with my straw, holding it in my mouth, then blowing it onto the table and making cool patterns on the table with the spilled liquid. It was okay because Mrs. Hauser was sitting on the other end of the table and couldn't see what I was doing.

Brittany's presents from Lauren and Paige were equally amazing — a suede iPod purse with Brittany's name written on it in gold, and a white leather belt with a rhinestone belt buckle and iPod holder right on it.

I was beginning to realize that my present — a book — was going to be totally out of place. I should have just done what my mom had said and explained that I'd be dropping off a present later next week when my parents got back from San Francisco.

Even Courtney's present, which wasn't iPod related, was better than mine: It was a pretty bracelet made out of purple crystals, which sparkled in the lights from The Cheesecake Factory ceiling. Everyone oohed and aahed as Brittany held it up.

"I got it when my family went to New York last Christmas," Courtney said. "It reminded me of you, Brittany."

Brittany looked really pleased. And why wouldn't she? Who wouldn't want a bracelet of purple crystals from New York City? I would.

Soon the only present left was mine. I felt sick to my stomach . . . and not just because my food had come, and the waitress had forgotten to write down the thing about the tomato. There was a big fat slice of one sitting right on my plate in front of me.

I wanted to pick it up and throw it on the floor for our dog, Marvin, to eat, like I would have done if we'd been at home.

But I wasn't at home, and Marvin wasn't there.

And besides, throwing food on the floor is bad manners.

That's a rule.

"Gee, I wonder what this could be," Brittany said as she lifted her last present.

Everyone laughed, because my present was obviously a book. You could tell by the shape.

Mrs. Hauser, digging into her gigantic lobster salad, said, "Now, Brittany," but not in a mean way. I wondered what Mr. Fernando was doing for his dinner, or if he had to wait in the car while we ate ours. Maybe I could bring him my cheeseburger. I didn't want it anymore, and not just because a tomato had touched it.

"Wow," Brittany said, after she'd torn the comic-paper wrapping off my present. "It's a book."

She didn't say it like, "Wow! It's a book!" She said it like, "Wow. It's a book." Like, what could be more boring than a book?

"It's a really good book," I said from where I sat, down the table from her. "*A Wrinkle in Time* is my favorite book ever. Have you read it?"

"No," Brittany said.

"It's really great," I said. "It's about a girl named Meg, and her father is missing, and her little brother, Charles Wallace, is a genius, only no one knows it, and this handsome boy from Meg's school comes over, and Meg has this huge crush on him, and —"

"Maybe I'll download the movie of it with my iTunes gift card," Brittany said unenthusiastically.

I felt my stomach lurch. See, there is no movie of *A*

Wrinkle in Time. Well, there is, but it was a TV movie, and it left out all the good parts from the book, like most movies made from books.

You can't watch the movie of *A Wrinkle in Time* and get the full effect of the book. You just can't.

Especially if you watch it on an *iPod*.

Brittany put down the book without even opening it to see where it said *To a true friend* inside, or reading the back to check what the book was about. Then she took a big bite of her cheeseburger — which had tomato on it — and said, with her mouth full, "Thanks, Allie."

But only because her mother was watching.

I could tell she didn't care about the book. I could tell she didn't care at all.

RULE #10

Sometimes, the Brave Thing to Do Is Go Home

I tried to eat my burger. I did. I nibbled the sides of it and ate a few fries.

But I'll be honest: Everything tasted like ashes. Not that I have ever eaten ashes. But that's how they say things taste in books.

And even though it wasn't true — everything actually tasted very delicious — that's how I *felt* like my dinner at The Cheesecake Factory tasted. Because of the company I was in. I didn't want to be there. I had made a huge mistake. I had missed the Little Miss Majorette Baton Twirling Twirltacular. I had given away the copy of *A Wrinkle in Time* that Harmony had given to me and had written *To a true friend* inside.

And for what?

So I could ride in a limo?

Riding in a limo wasn't all that great, actually.

To go to Glitterati?

Going to Glitterati hadn't been all that great, either.

To eat at The Cheesecake Factory?

Well, The Cheesecake Factory was good and all, except for the tomato on my plate and the fact that the people I was with were totally horrible.

I wanted to cry. I really did. I was miserable. I was having the worst time of my entire life.

In fact, by the time the cake came — a huge Godiva chocolate cheesecake, with sparklers on it; the entire staff of The Cheesecake Factory, it seemed like, came out and sang a very happy Cheesecake Factory birthday to Brittany. I thought her face was going to break in two, she loved the attention so much — I thought I was going to cry for real, in front of all of them, the well of my sorrow was so deep. I had to excuse myself and go to the ladies' room. I just needed to be alone for a minute to collect my thoughts.

But The Cheesecake Factory's ladies' room was the wrong place to go to be alone. There were tons of people in there. There were moms changing their babies' diapers and teenage girls complaining to each other about their boyfriends. There were ladies talking on their cell phones and other ladies holding their beepers, wondering when they were going to go off and when they were going to get a table. I had to wiggle my way past all of them to find a stall. Finally, I found one and closed the door and sat there, trying not to cry.

I wished the toilet stall I was sitting in was a time portal and I could close my eyes and use it to travel back through time to this morning in the driveway and come out of it and do everything differently. I would have gotten into the minivan with Erica and those guys and gone to the Twirltacular instead of to Glitterati. Uncle Jay could have explained to Mrs. Hauser when the limo showed up that I was sick or something. That would have been a better lie than the one I gave my friends about my mom making me go to Brittany's birthday party or she'd lose her job.

Because I don't even care about Brittany and those guys, and I actually care about my friends.

But unfortunately, the toilet stall wasn't a time portal. I could tell because when I opened my eyes, I was still in it. And I could still hear all the Cheesecake Factory ladies complaining about how come their beepers weren't going off.

In *A Wrinkle in Time*, you can create a thing called a tesseract . . . a wrinkle in time to get from one place to another in the blink of an eye.

I wished I could create a tesseract and go home. Right at that moment.

If only tesseracts were real.

After a little while, I figured I better come out of the bathroom, or Mrs. Hauser might start to wonder where I was (I didn't think Brittany or her friends would care). I flushed and came out to wash my hands.

Nothing could have startled me more when I was drying them than seeing Courtney standing there, looking at me. Like she'd been waiting for me!

"Hi," she said. "I just wanted to see if you were okay."

I couldn't believe it. She had been waiting for me! Someone cared! Someone actually cared about me!

"Um," I said, walking away from the hand blower. "Thanks. I thought . . . I thought you hated me. Like all the rest of them."

"No," Courtney said. "We're friends. Remember?"

And she pulled out the necklace she'd been messing around with all day. On the end of the silver chain was half a heart. A broken heart.

That's when I remembered . . .

. . . I had the other half. Courtney had given it to me, my last day of school at Walnut Knolls. I'd totally forgotten about that. I'd just moved and never given it another thought.

Now I felt like a jerk.

Because all this time, Courtney had been my friend, wearing the other half of a broken-heart necklace. And I had never called her or tried to see her since I'd moved away from Walnut Knolls. Not once in all this time.

"Oh, Courtney," I said. "Of course." I didn't tell her I'd forgotten. Because that would have hurt her feelings. "I thought . . . I thought maybe things had changed, and you were friends with Brittany now."

"No," Courtney said, and gave a little shudder. It was kind of hard to talk in The Cheesecake Factory's ladies' room, because so many people were coming in and out, and they were playing the music so loud in there. Plus there was the near constant sound of the hand blowers.

But we found a little corner where there was a black leather bench and sat down on it.

"I still hang out with Brittany," Courtney explained, "but ever since she started being best friends with Mary Kay instead of me, she kind of treats me like her dog. She's always like, Go get me this, and Go get me that."

I widened my eyes. "Then why do you hang out with her?" I asked.

"Well, because if it weren't for her, I wouldn't have any friends at all," Courtney said simply.

I felt doubly sorry after that that I hadn't called Courtney since I'd moved. Not everyone could be like me — I mean, a strong person who would stand up to someone who put her down, like I had with Brittany and then Cheyenne O'Malley.

"Wow," I said. "I'm really sorry, Courtney."

I wasn't sure if she knew what I was saying sorry for. I wasn't sure I knew myself. It was true I hadn't called Courtney since I'd moved — but then, she hadn't called me, either.

"It's okay," Courtney said with a shrug. "Brittany's kind of mean, but at least she's not boring, like Mary Kay."

That was definitely true.

"And Paige and Lauren can be all right," she went on.

"I just don't get," I said, "why she invited me to her party when she seems to hate me so much."

"Oh, that," Courtney said. "Everybody wants to be friends with you because of your mom being on that TV show. And you moving to that new school, and having that big new house, and going with boys, and all of that."

I rolled my eyes.

"Courtney," I said. "None of that stuff is true. I mean, it's true my mom is on a TV show, but she doesn't even get paid for it. And my new school isn't really that different from Walnut Knolls, except that it's really old, and my new house is really old, too, and the boy who asked me to go with him . . . he's nice, and everything, but . . . the truth is, he likes to bark instead of talk, and he hardly ever remembers to wash his face in the morning."

Courtney looked like she wanted to laugh but was afraid to. "No way . . . really?"

"Really," I said. "I think people have been making my life sound way more glamorous than it really is."

"They have," Courtney said. "And Brittany is really jealous. That's why she started being so mean to you. She couldn't stand hearing about you having a boy ask you out, and you actually turning him down. It made her so green with envy, she started trying to make you have a bad time at her party, first by forcing you to dress as a pirate, then telling you you looked dumb, then saying she never told you that, then by making fun of your gift. It will probably get worse as the night goes on."

This made my eyes bug out.

"Really?" I asked. I couldn't imagine it getting worse. Unless Brittany planned on murdering me.

"Yeah," Courtney said, with a nod. "After you left to go to the bathroom, I heard Brittany telling Mary Kay and those guys that tonight in the hotel, after you fall asleep, she's going to stick your hand in a glass of hot water to make you wet the bed."

My eyes got even wider. How had I gotten into this mess?

"It's true," Courtney said. "And after that, they're going to get a red pen from her mom's purse and draw little spots all over your face, so that when you wake up, you'll think you have pimples."

I threw my hands over my face. This was awful! Now, just because Brittany was jealous over my relationship with Joey Fields — *Joey Fields!* — I was going to get humiliated in the night while I slept! Who knew what else Brittany might be planning right now, as Courtney and I were talking.

Well, I wasn't going to just sit here and take it.

And unlike last time, I wasn't going to make the mistake of telling on Brittany, either. I had learned my lesson with the thing with Lady Serena Archibald. I was going to handle this situation on my own.

With a little help from my friends, of course.

Because suddenly, I had realized something:

There was *such a thing as a tesseract.*

Well, sort of.

"Courtney," I said. "Can I borrow your cell phone?"

"Sure," she said, looking surprised. She dug around for it in her purse. "But who are you going to call?"

"Home," I said.

As soon as he picked up the phone, I said, "Uncle Jay?"

"Allie?" Uncle Jay sounded out of breath. That, I realized, was because he'd had to run from the living room, where he'd set up the tent, to get to the phone in the kitchen. Still, he sounded cheerful, like they were having a good time. And why wouldn't they be? They were having a cookout in the living room. "Hey! How's it going?"

"Not very good," I said. "I need you to come pick me up."

Uncle Jay stopped sounding so cheerful.

"What? Why? Are you all right?"

"No," I said. "Brittany and her friends are being really mean to me. They're going to do some really mean stuff to me tonight after I fall asleep. And I need you to come get me."

"Allie," Uncle Jay said, "I can't come get you. You're all the way in the city. That's an hour away. And I've got Mark and Kevin here. I can't drop everything and drive all the way up there just because some of your girlfriends are picking on you."

This was the last thing I expected to hear from Uncle Jay. He had always been there for me!

"Uncle Jay," I said, turning away from Courtney, so she couldn't hear me. Or see the tears that were filling up in my eyes. "I don't think you understand. It's bad. Really bad. I made a big mistake coming here. And I need someone to come get me before things get even worse."

"Can't someone there drive you back?" Uncle Jay wanted to know. "Mrs. Hauser?"

"No," I said. "Nobody is coming back until tomorrow morning. And by tomorrow morning, I'll be dead."

There was silence on the line. It was kind of hard to tell if he was still even on the line, because of all the music in the bathroom and the ladies talking and the beepers going off and the hand blowers and everything.

But I could faintly hear the sounds of Mark and Kevin in the background, fighting over who got to hold the stick for the marshmallows for the s'mores.

They were roasting marshmallows over the fire in the fireplace for s'mores? No fair!

I wished I was home more than ever now.

"Well," Uncle Jay finally said, "I guess I could call Harmony. If she doesn't have too much studying to do, maybe she could come get you."

"Uncle Jay," I said, my heart feeling like it was about to pound out of my chest, I was so happy. "If Harmony could do that, I would be so forever grateful to her. I would do anything you say for the rest of your life. I would make all the pizzas for Pizza Express forever. . . ."

"I think that would be a violation of child labor laws," Uncle Jay said, maybe remembering how the pizza I'd made last night had turned out kind of number eight–shaped and not really round. "But you would definitely owe me. And Harmony. Because she has way better things to do than drive up to the city and pick up confused little girls who don't know who their real friends are."

"That is so me," I said sadly. "I deserve to be called that."

"You do," Uncle Jay said. He didn't sound at all happy with me. "Also, I'm going to have to give her some of your mom's money for gas. So that means we're going to have to eat Hot Pockets all day tomorrow. Anyway. Where should she pick you up?"

"The hotel lobby," I said. "I'll be waiting for her."

"Okay," Uncle Jay said. "And, Allie, you owe me for this one."

"I owe you so many times over," I said. "Uncle Jay, you're my tesseract."

"Your what?"

"My tesseract."

"Whatever, kid," he said.

And hung up.

Then I handed the phone back to Courtney.

It was only then that I noticed she looked like she wanted to cry.

"So," she said as she glumly slipped her phone back into her purse. "You're going to go home."

"Um, yeah," I said. All my excitement over knowing I was getting out of this bad situation disappeared. I felt terrible for ditching Courtney.

Then I had an idea.

"Hey," I said. "My uncle's girlfriend is coming to pick me up. Do you want to come home with me? You could spend the night. I'm sure he'd say it was okay. You could call your mom and ask."

"No," Courtney said sadly. "It's all right for you. You never have to see Brittany again if you don't want to. You get to go back to your new school and see all your new friends on Monday morning. But I have to see those same girls every day. If I leave, they'd never stop torturing me. So I better stay."

I felt bad, hearing Courtney say all that. It was true, though. Her staying and facing her problems was the best thing she could do.

Courtney was a way braver person than I was. I really admired her for that. I decided I wanted to be more like her.

But for now, I was getting my tesseract and taking it the heck out of there.

Because sometimes, the brave thing to do is go home. That's a rule.

"Well," I said. "I promise you, when this is all over, I'm going to have you over to my new house, and you're going to see my life isn't as great as Brittany and those guys think. But we're going to have a blast."

"Okay," Courtney said. But she didn't look like she believed me. "I better get back out there. What do you want me to tell them?"

"Tell them I'm sick," I said.

"But . . ." Courtney looked at me funny. "You aren't sick."

"Oh," I said confidentially. "I will be."

RULE #11

Always Be True to Your Friends, Just as You Are to Yourself

Part of preparing to have a future career as an actress slash veterinarian — besides reading every book you can find in your school library about animals — is that you have to be ready for every acting challenge that comes along. Not just getting a part that you don't necessarily want, like a role that's maybe a little less glamorous than the lead.

But playing a part in real life, such as the part of yourself, only being sick to your stomach from something you ate at Brittany Hauser's birthday dinner, so that you had to call your uncle's girlfriend to come get you.

So instead of going up with the rest of the girls to the hotel room Mrs. Hauser got for them, you have to sit in the lobby and wait for your uncle's girlfriend to come pick you up.

This is called *acting*. It's very difficult.

I didn't want to have to do this whole fake-sick thing, but it wasn't like I had any choice. I knew Brittany's intentions: to put my hand in a glass of warm water, thus making me wet the bed, and to put red spots all over my face, using a red pen from Mrs. Hauser's purse, all while I slept.

How did I know the ink from that pen wouldn't give me ink poisoning, something Sophie once warned me had caused a kid in England to die?

And what if I was somehow electrocuted from the water they stuck my hand into? Everyone knows water plus electricity equals death. Sophie had told me all about that.

Asleep, I wouldn't be able to protect myself from either of these things. I was in a life-and-death situation.

Therefore, acting was called for.

That's why, as soon as Courtney left, I turned on one of the hand blowers and swung the nozzle thingie so that it was blowing onto my forehead. I stuck my head there and let it blow for as long as I could stand it.

Then I walked over to the mirror and fixed my hair — which had gotten pretty messy, from being blown around — and felt my own forehead.

Perfect.

Then I practiced looking sick. It wasn't hard. I had barely eaten anything all day except Coke and caramel corn and a few fries. I *felt* a little sick.

A few minutes later, Mrs. Hauser came into the ladies' room, looking worried.

"Allie," she said. "Courtney says you aren't feeling well."

"I'm really not," I said from the black leather bench, where I'd gone to slump like a sick person.

Mrs. Hauser felt my forehead.

"Oh, my," she said. "You do feel a little warm."

"Yes, ma'am," I said faintly. "My stomach hurts a little, too. If it's okay, I already used Courtney's phone to call my uncle. He's going to have his girlfriend, Harmony, pick me up in the hotel lobby. I'm really sorry to spoil Brittany's birthday."

I liked that line, *I'm really sorry to spoil Brittany's birthday.* It had taken me a little while to come up with it. It seemed like the kind of thing a person who was really sick might say.

And while I was sorry for lying to Mrs. Hauser, because she had always been really, really nice to me, being Mewsie's grandma and all, I wasn't sorry at all about potentially spoiling Brittany's birthday. Because I knew I wasn't really spoiling Brittany's birthday. Brittany could not have cared less that I was leaving her birthday party early. She was probably happy to be getting rid of me.

Except for the part where she wasn't going to get to torture me in my sleep. That part of her birthday really was ruined for her.

"Oh, you poor thing," Mrs. Hauser said, giving me a hug. "Don't you worry about Brittany. I'll make sure we get you to the hotel soon so you can meet — what's her name?"

"Harmony," I said.

"Harmony. Of course. Do you think you can make it back to the table without . . . ?"

She wanted to say "throwing up" without actually saying it, because she was afraid saying it might make me do it. Which it usually does, for people who are really sick. It's a rule.

"Yes, ma'am," I said again, all faintly. I let Mrs. Hauser lead me back to the table, keeping my face arranged in the way I thought a sick person might look. It totally worked, too, because people moved out of our way as we walked back to the alcove where Brittany's birthday table was. That hand blower trick had actually worked. I looked all feverish and sweaty.

"Well, girls," Mrs. Hauser said, as she guided me to my seat, "I'm afraid Allie isn't feeling well and is going to have to go home early."

"Awww," Brittany and her friends said, in very fakey voices. They didn't care that I was sick. They were just disappointed that they weren't going to have me around to play their mean pranks on later.

All except Courtney. She actually seemed upset.

She knew I wasn't really sick, though. She didn't want me to leave her alone with Brittany and her friends.

I felt bad for her, but what could I do? I had to get out of there.

When we got to the hotel and Mrs. Hauser picked up the keys to the rooms where she and the girls were going to stay, Brittany and Mary Kay and Paige and Lauren made a big deal out of saying good-bye to me in the lobby. Brittany especially. She gave me this big hug and said in a really fake voice, "I'm so sorry you got sick, Allie. I hope you feel better soon."

Mrs. Hauser poked her, and Brittany went, "Oh, yeah. And thanks for the *book*."

Mary Kay, Paige, and Lauren all snickered.

You could tell Brittany didn't like the book I'd given her, and that she had no intention of ever opening it up to read it. Any more than she cared that I was sick (even though I wasn't) and leaving her party early.

She was such a stuck-up snob. All she cared about was getting up to the hotel room. In the back of the limo on the way from the restaurant, she and Mary Kay and those guys couldn't stop talking about the pranks they were going to play when they got there, such as calling other rooms and asking them if they would like a prank call played on them (and then when the caller said no, they were going to scream, "Well, you just did!" and hang up), and sneaking out of the room and pouring water over the atrium railing onto the unsuspecting heads of passersby in the lobby many stories below.

These sorts of pranks were, I knew, illegal. Or, if not illegal, probably very much frowned upon by the hotel staff. I felt sorry for Courtney, who was going to have to go along with them, or be cruelly shunned by the group if she didn't. I was more glad than ever that my parents had forced me to move from the Walnut Knolls school district, even though I hadn't liked it at the time, to the Pine Heights school district, where there was a higher quality of student.

Courtney said a very sad good-bye to me in the lobby, even though she couldn't express her true emotions in front of Brittany and the others, because then they'd suspect something. She went, "Bye, Allie."

And I said, "Bye."

But our eyes spoke eloquently of our true emotions.

So now I was sitting on an elegant brown suede bench in the lobby of the luxury Hilton Hotel, waiting for Harmony to come rescue me, while Mrs. Hauser talked to the concierge . . . whatever that was . . . about how the room Brittany and those guys were staying in wasn't right next door to hers, and that was unacceptable. How was Mrs. Hauser going to keep an eye on them if her room wasn't right next door? Yes, she realized they were just little girls and couldn't get up to much trouble, but it was her responsibility.

Meanwhile, the bellman had all the luggage from the limo piled up on a big cart and was about to take it upstairs. The book Harmony had given me, *A Wrinkle in Time*, was sticking out of the Glitterati bag where Brittany had thrown it (Mrs. Hauser had let Brittany buy her urban fairy outfit from Glitterati. I had no idea where Brittany thought she was going to wear a pair of skintight jeans and a sparkle halter top. School? Knowing Brittany, probably so).

I don't know what came over me, really. I was supposed to be sitting there, *not moving* (according to Mrs. Hauser), until Harmony came.

But instead, quick as I could, I got up and ran over to the luggage cart and grabbed the copy of *A Wrinkle in Time*, then darted back to my seat and stuffed the book into my backpack.

I looked over to see if Mrs. Hauser had noticed.

But she hadn't.

I'd done it! I'd gotten my book back! My heart was beating really fast. I couldn't believe what I'd done. I'd stolen back my gift to Brittany.

I wasn't sorry, either. Brittany didn't deserve such a nice gift. A present should come from the heart, Uncle Jay had said.

Well, Harmony had given me this present, from her heart. I was *not* giving it to Brittany. Not anymore. Not after I'd seen how she'd treated it. It was too nice a gift for Brittany. Let my mom go out and get Brittany some gift certificate or something. That was all she deserved.

Not something as nice as my favorite book of all time.

It was right then that I heard a familiar voice say, "Allie?" and I looked up, and there was Harmony, wearing a bright green raincoat and walking toward me through the hotel's atrium, looking fresh and pretty and confused and basically like the most beautiful thing I had ever seen in my whole entire life.

In fact, I was so happy to see her, I jumped up from the bench I was sitting on and ran to her, throwing my arms around her waist and hugging her as hard as I could.

A sick person probably wouldn't act like this, but I didn't care anymore.

My tesseract had come through for me.

"Oh, my goodness, Allie," Harmony said, hugging me back. "Are you all right? Jay said you —"

"Oh, hello," Mrs. Hauser said, coming over with her right hand outstretched. "You must be Harmony?"

"I am," Harmony said, and shook Mrs. Hauser's hand.

"Allie's not feeling well," Mrs. Hauser said. "I'm so glad you could come pick her up. I'm sure she must be disappointed to have to leave the party so early, but she felt so feverish. I hope it isn't that flu that's going around. I really didn't want her to give it to the rest of the girls. . . ."

I let go of Harmony and stood there, trying to look

feverish. For a person with my vast amount of acting experience, this wasn't hard.

"Uh," Harmony said. "I understand. Thanks a lot for looking out for her."

"Oh, it wasn't any problem," Mrs. Hauser said. "Allie's such a joy to have around."

Another person who thought I was a joy to have around! Mrs. Hunter wasn't the only one!

And I didn't think Mrs. Hauser was only saying that because she wanted to make sure she didn't get in trouble with my mom, who is a local celebrity, for letting me get sick while she was watching me. Mrs. Hauser and I do share a special bond, since we're both cat lovers.

"Okay, then," Harmony said to Mrs. Hauser. "I won't keep you from your daughter's party. I guess we should go. Allie, do you have all your stuff?"

I had my backpack — with the birthday gift I'd stolen back safely hidden in it — and my wheelie bag. I nodded, and Harmony said, "Let's go. Nice meeting you, Mrs. Hauser."

"Thank you very much, Mrs. Hauser," I said, one last time. "I'm sorry to have been such a bother."

"Oh, Allie," Mrs. Hauser said, cupping my face in her hands and smiling down at me. "Don't even think twice about it."

Harmony took hold of the handle of my wheelie bag and the two of us walked through the hotel lobby, past the huge waterfall that Kevin loved so much, and past the glass elevators that led up to the floor where I knew Brittany and her friends were staying. When I turned my head to look back at Mrs. Hauser, still feeling a bit bad about lying to her, I actually thought I saw five little heads peering down at me from one of the glass elevator cars as it shot smoothly up toward the big glass ceiling.

But that had to have been my imagination. Mrs. Hauser had told the girls to stay in their room, and not to go creeping around the hotel while she was downstairs.

Surely, Brittany wouldn't have disobeyed her mother *now*, when Mrs. Hauser wasn't even asleep yet. . . .

Oh. Right. Of course she had.

"So," Harmony said as we walked through the automatic doors to the parking lot, where she'd left her car. "What's going on? Why am I here? You're not really sick, are you?"

"Well," I said. It was cold outside. Also, it was lightly raining, and it had gotten dark. "Not really . . ."

And as we began the long drive home, I told Harmony everything that had happened.

We drove along the highway very fast (though of course obeying the speed limit), with Harmony's music playing on the CD player (she liked to listen to female folk rock), and I told her what had happened, starting at the beginning, about how I'd wanted to go to Missy's Little Miss Majorette Baton Twirling Twirltacular, but how I'd chosen instead to go to Brittany's birthday party.

I didn't mention the part about how I'd lied to them about my mom forcing me to go to Brittany's party or *Good News!* would lose all its advertising money. I had the feeling Harmony would be pretty upset if she heard about that, and might make me do something stupid like confess to

Erica and those guys that I'd been lying . . . not to mention to my mom.

Instead, I went on to tell Harmony how I'd then been forced to lie to Mrs. Hauser that I was sick in order to get out of having to spend the night with Brittany and *her* friends, and how mean they'd been to me (all except Courtney), and what had happened at Glitterati, and then at The Cheesecake Factory, and how Brittany had said I'd looked dumb and then denied it, and how Courtney had said they were going to put my hand in warm water and then draw dots on my face, and how I'd had to fake being sick to get out of there.

The only thing I didn't tell Harmony (besides the lie about Mom) was about the book, because I didn't want Harmony to know that I'd almost given the book she'd given to me away as a gift to someone else.

When I was done telling her why I'd called Uncle Jay and asked him to come pick me up — and why he'd called her and asked her to do it for him — Harmony just stared thoughtfully out the windshield at the highway in front of us.

"So," she said finally. "You ended up at a birthday party full of mean girls."

"Yes," I said.

"When you could," she said, "have spent the day at a baton-twirling competition with your real, nice friends."

"Yes," I said. It was embarrassing but true.

"So, you made some very bad choices," Harmony said.

"Yes," I said. "But I realized it. Just in time."

"Not really in time," Harmony said. "Because you greatly inconvenienced me by taking two hours out of my life to have to drive to the city to get you and then drive you back."

I swallowed hard. There was a very big lump in my throat.

"I'm really, really sorry about that," I said.

"And," Harmony went on, "you still got to do the things you wanted to do — ride in a limo and go to Glitterati. And you still probably disappointed your friend Erica by not being there for her sister, Missy."

Now that Harmony had pointed it out, I realized again how really, truly selfish I had been.

"Yes," I said for a fourth time. "I'm a really bad friend."

"Well," Harmony said. "The good thing is, you know it. So maybe there's still time for you to fix it."

"I don't see how," I sobbed.

"Why don't you give your friend Erica a call," Harmony said, "when you get home, and see how her sister did in her competition today?"

"That's a good idea," I said. It was hard to talk with my nose running so badly from all the crying.

But Harmony had made an excellent point. Maybe there was still time to fix things with Erica.

Harmony was mad about having to take two hours out of her own time to come pick me up in the city and drive me back . . . but not so mad that she didn't pull into a McDonald's and buy us both dinner. She said all girls made mistakes sometimes, and that it was lucky for me I had a cool uncle who had a cool girlfriend to bail me out of this one.

She was right. I was pretty sure if it had been my mom I'd called, she'd have made me stay at the birthday party, to learn from my mistake. Like I hadn't learned from it already. A lot.

I really did have the coolest uncle — who had the coolest girlfriend — in the world. Harmony didn't even say anything when I made the McDonald's people special-order my burger so it didn't have ketchup on it, and it took an extra seven minutes to be ready.

As soon as Harmony parked in our driveway, I got out of her car, grabbed my wheelie bag and backpack, and went inside, more glad than I could ever remember feeling to be home.

"I'm home!" I yelled as soon as I got into the mudroom.

"We're in here!" I heard Kevin and Mark scream. I put my stuff down and followed the sound of their voices to the living room. There I met with the sight of our family tent, bathed in the glow of a roaring fire in our fireplace, and Uncle Jay, Mark, and Kevin, each dressed in cowboy gear, roasting marshmallows over the open flames.

"Oh," Harmony said, when she saw that the mantel Mom had carefully restored was singed black from the flames. "You are going to get it when your brother and sister-in-law come home."

"Yeah," Uncle Jay said. "Well, the flames really weren't hot enough to cook hot dogs over, so I added some charcoal and lighter fluid, and things got a little out of hand. But I'll scrape all that off after it cools down, and they'll never know the difference. Hi, Allie!"

"Hi," I said. "You guys look like you're having a good time."

"The best time ever," Mark said.

"I'm a pirate cowboy," Kevin said. He was, indeed, wearing a cowboy hat with the rest of his pirate outfit.

"Wow," I said. "That reminds me. I have something to show you later. But I have to go call someone first."

I left them enjoying their cowboy booty and went to the kitchen phone. I have to admit, my heart was beating kind of fast. What if Erica didn't want to talk to me? What if she hung up when she heard it was me, because I'd chosen Glitterati over her sister's twirling meet?

I had to take the risk.

I pressed the button that speed-dialed the Harringtons'

house. It was late to be calling, it was true, but only a little after nine. Hopefully, no one would be too mad.

"Hello?" a boy's voice said. It was John.

"Hello," I said. "This is Allie Finkle. May I please speak to Erica?"

"I don't know, Allie Finkle," John said. "Erica's pretty mad at you for not coming to Missy's Twirltacular today."

Oh, no! This was awful! My heart started beating faster than ever.

"Really?" My hand that was clutching the phone started to feel really sweaty.

"Yeah," John said. "I heard her and her friends saying they never wanted to speak to you again."

Oh! This was exactly what I'd been afraid would happen.

"I —" I didn't know what to say. "I — I'm calling to say I'm sorry," I said. "I —"

Then I heard Erica yell, "John!" and in the background, someone started yelling. I thought it was Erica. John started laughing and saying, "Get off me!" and then there were a lot of breathing and grunting sounds like the phone was being wrestled away from him.

Finally, I heard Erica yell, "Mom! The phone is for me, and John won't give it to me!"

And Mrs. Harrington said, "John! Do we have to discuss this again?"

And John said, "I was just messing with her," and then Erica's voice came on the phone, loud and clear, if slightly breathless, going, "Allie? Allie, is that you?"

"Erica?" I couldn't believe, after what John had said, that she was actually speaking to me. "Erica, I just called to say I'm so, so sorry about what happened. I made such a mistake going to that girl's stupid birthday party instead of to your sister's Twirltacular, and I really, really hope you'll forgive me and be my friend again someday. Because I learned my lesson. You're the best friend I've ever had, and I would never want to do anything to jeopardize our friendship."

"Allie!" Erica cried. "What are you talking about? Did you have fun at the party? What was Glitterati like? And riding in the limo? Are you calling from the hotel now?"

"No," I said, laughing. I was so relieved to hear Erica's voice, I wanted to cry all over again. But this time with happiness. "It was awful. It was so terrible, I pretended to get sick and I left! I made Uncle Jay send Harmony to pick me up. And, Erica, that thing, about my mom and her job? It was all a misunderstanding."

"Oh," Erica said. "Really?"

"Yes," I said. "And another thing. I realized that what Sophie said was right. Riding in a limo and going to Glitterati and things like that are only fun to do if you do them with your real friends . . . with people like you."

"Oh," Erica said. "Well, I hope I get to do those things with you someday. But I don't think I'd ever get to do those kinds of things for my birthday, because we aren't rich, like the Hausers. My mom usually just makes a cake and we have a sleepover and watch a movie and maybe tell scary stories."

"Me, too," I said. I was so busy wiping away my tears of happiness that I didn't even realize I'd wiped too hard and rubbed off my stick-on tear of infinite sorrow.

But when I saw it stuck to my finger, I didn't put it back on my face. I realized I didn't need it anymore.

"I'd rather have cake and a sleepover with you than go to Glitterati any day," I said. "So, how did Missy do at the Little Miss Majorette Baton Twirling Twirltacular?"

"Oh, she did so great," Erica said. "She made it to the finals! They're tomorrow. Do you want to come watch?"

My heart, which I didn't think could have taken much more excitement, seemed to explode with happiness in my chest.

"There are more rounds tomorrow?" I asked. "You mean, I didn't miss the whole thing?"

"Oh, of course not," Erica said. "We're all going back tomorrow to support Missy in the solo and dance finals. It would be great if you could come, Allie. Do you think you can?"

"I *know* I can," I said. "But first . . . is it okay if I bring something over?"

"Bring something over? To my house? Right now?"

"You live right next door," I reminded her. "I'll only be a minute."

"I'm in my pajamas already," Erica said, laughing. "But sure."

I hung up the phone.

"I just have to run next door to Erica's for a second," I yelled to everyone in the living room.

Harmony was trying to blow out the flames on Kevin's marshmallow, which were out of control.

"Be *right* back," she said.

"I will!" I said.

I loved having Uncle Jay and Harmony, the coolest babysitters in the world, taking care of us.

I ran outside into the cool night air, cut through our front yard and the hedge that separates our yard from the alley beside it, then crossed the alley and dived through the hedge that lets me into the Harringtons' front yard. No one was outside because it was too rainy and dark out.

But it was fun being out so late . . . even if it wasn't *so* late. I mean, Mrs. Shipley from down the street was out, walking her dog. She waved to me, and I waved back.

I ran up onto the Harringtons' porch. Erica was already at the door, waiting for me, with the light on. She was in her white flannel nightgown with the blue butterflies on it.

"Allie," she said, looking confused. "What's going on?"

"Here," I said, passing her something. "This is for you."

Erica looked down at the book I'd given her.

"*A Wrinkle in Time*?" She smiled. "This is the book Mrs. Hunter read to us in class. It's your favorite, isn't it?"

"Yes," I said. "Look what's written on the inside."

Erica opened it. "*To a true friend,*" she read. She looked back up at me, smiling, tears in her eyes. "Thanks, Allie. That's so sweet. But . . . it's not my birthday."

"I know," I said. "But I want you to have it. Because presents should come from the heart. And you deserve it." I gave her a quick hug. "Good night!"

Then I turned and ran back home.

RULE #12

Practice Makes Perfect

The Little Miss Majorette Baton Twirling Twirltacular was exactly how Erica had described it to me. Only better.

It was packed with people, just like The Cheesecake Factory had been.

Except these people weren't waiting for their beepers to go off so they could get their tables and sit down to have some delicious food.

These people were there to see girls (and some boys) compete in the middle school division of the state baton-twirling competition. Almost all the bleachers in the gymnasium were full.

But since we got there early, we got seats very close to the front, so we could see everything going on on the blue mats in front of us.

"Today we'll be seeing the best in dance, strut, teams, showtwirls, solos, multiple batons, flags, hoops, and duets/ pairs," Erica explained to me as I sat with her, Sophie, and Caroline. Mr. and Mrs. Harrington were sitting farther up the bleachers. John was sitting with some girls a few sets of bleachers away. He'd met some older girl twirlers yesterday, Erica explained, and now he was pretending he didn't know anyone in the Harrington family.

This, Erica said, was normal for teenage boys.

The best in dance, strut, teams, showtwirls, solos, multiple batons, flags, hoops, and duets/pairs really took my breath away. The girls (and some boys) were so good! They tossed and twirled and danced and did things with batons that I would never have thought possible, based on the laws of gravity. They had all practiced really, really hard.

The Little Miss Majorette Baton Twirling Twirltacular was better, I decided, than Glitterati. Because even though it's fun to envision your future sometimes, and dress up as what you want to be, and get your picture taken looking all glamorous, it was more fun to watch people who were actually *living* their future.

It was so exciting when the music started to play and the twirlers came out with their beautiful costumes and their batons and their big bright smiles. It made your heart beat a little bit faster when you saw them turn and face the judges.

Because it wasn't people *pretending* to be good at something, like at Glitterati. There was nothing fake about the Little Miss Majorette Baton Twirling Twirltacular.

It was 100 percent real.

And I loved it.

Just like Erica, Sophie, and Caroline loved my photo from Glitterati.

"A pirate!" Sophie cried. "I've never in my life heard of a fourth-grade girl going to Glitterati and dressing as a pirate!"

"Allie," Caroline said, shaking her head. "You are such a geek!"

But she meant it in a nice way. Soon we were all laughing at my picture . . . and my stories about Brittany's horrible birthday party (I explained to Sophie and Caroline about the "misunderstanding" concerning my mom and her job, too, just so everyone understood). That's what we were talking about when a fifth girl walked up to us.

"Allie?" she said.

"Oh!" I broke off laughing. "Everyone, this is my friend Courtney. I hope you don't mind, but I asked her to spend the afternoon with me." I stood up and showed them all the half of the broken-heart necklace I was wearing, and how it matched Courtney's. "Courtney's a good friend of mine from my old school."

Courtney blushed, I guess from seeing that I was finally wearing the necklace she'd given me so long ago. "Hi," she said to my friends.

"Hi, Courtney," they all said, and scooted over to make room for her on the bench.

I was glad Courtney had come to the Twirltacular. When I'd called her on her cell phone that morning, she'd said the slumber party had been a bust. After they'd made a few prank calls, Brittany had made the girls play truth or dare, and she'd ended up daring Mary Kay to sneak out into the atrium and pour a can of 7UP onto the heads of some people standing in the lobby below their twelfth-floor room.

Only it turned out the people Mary Kay had poured the soda on had been some police officers.

And they hadn't liked Brittany's little prank very much. In fact, they'd figured out which room the girls were in, and gone up there and banged on the door and woken Mrs. Hauser up. In the morning, Mrs. Hauser and all the girls were told to pack their stuff and leave. Before brunch!

None of the Hausers was welcome to check into any of the hotels owned by the Hilton family ever again.

But Courtney hadn't minded because it meant she got to go home early.

I almost wished I could have been there to see the angry policemen.

"Policewomen," Courtney corrected me. "They were policewomen."

That just made the story even *better*.

"Wait," Erica said, grabbing my arm. "It's Missy's turn!"

And suddenly, the first few strains of "I'm Gonna Knock You Out" came on over the loudspeakers, and out marched Missy.

I don't know about anybody else, but I was holding my breath as I watched Missy prance forward in her rainbow leotard with all the spangles, then begin her solo, keeping a big smile plastered on her face even as she tossed her baton high, high, high into the air. It soared so close to the gymnasium's rafters, I was sure it would get stuck and she'd never be able to catch it. Down below, Missy was doing backflips as smoothly as a dolphin cutting through water, not even seeming to care that her baton was tumbling around up there in the air . . .

. . . and then, suddenly, she came out of one of her tumbles, and *bam* —

Just like that, she stuck out one hand and caught her baton . . .

. . . then kept *right on tumbling*, like it was nothing at all.

I couldn't help it. I screamed and jumped up to my feet, clapping as hard as I could, even though Missy had that *no talking* rule in her room. I wanted to cry. Not because I was sad, for once, but because it was all so amazing. I had seen Missy attempt that move hundreds of times — maybe even ten thousand times — in her front yard, and miss it.

But today, when it counted, she had done it perfectly.

And she had done it so amazingly well, right in time with the music, like someone on TV or in the Olympics or something. I had never seen anything like it.

And it had happened right here, right in front of me, in my very own town!

I guess my excitement was contagious, because everyone else in my row jumped to their feet and started clapping, too. I mean, it really *was* incredible.

"How did she do that?" Courtney whispered to me as she clapped.

How *could* someone do that, be spinning and flipping and dancing all around the gym, while her baton was flying through the air above her head, and then just reach out at the exact right moment and grab it? There was really only one explanation.

"Practice," I told her. "Lots and lots of practice."

"That's so neat," Courtney said. "It's so cool that you know her."

"I know," I said, and felt sort of proud. It was easy to forget all the times Missy had sat on me or slammed a door in my face when she was flipping around that mat in time to "I'm Gonna Knock You Out," making that baton do exactly what she was telling it to, without a single mistake.

By the time she was done, the whole gymnasium, practically, was on its feet, screaming.

And then the music ended, and Missy fell to one knee in her final pose, her hands stretched to the ceiling as her baton, shining like my pirate sword from Glitterati, tumbled down right into them. She didn't even look to make sure it was where she wanted it to be. She just *knew* that's where her baton was going to end up, in her hands.

And it did.

The applause was so loud, I thought the ceiling of the middle school was going to cave in.

"She's won for sure," I leaned over to say to Erica.

"Oh, I hope so!" Erica was clapping harder than anyone.

"She has to have won," Sophie yelled, to be heard over all the applause. "That was amazing! Your sister is so talented!"

"It's no wonder she's so moody," Caroline said. "She has the soul of a true artist."

Missy took her baton, gave a quick, professional bow, and walked off toward where her coach was standing, to wait for her scores. The crowd was still going wild. Everyone was waiting to see what the judges were going to give her.

But Sophie was right. Missy did win. She got a perfect score for the middle school ladies' solo event.

Her statue with the little gold baton-twirling lady on it ended up being as tall as I was.

"Wow," Courtney said, about Missy's trophy. "She's really lucky."

"No." I shook my head. "Luck had nothing to do with it. It was practice. She practiced every day. Sometimes even in the dark. Her mom would come out and yell at her."

"Wow," Courtney said again, impressed.

I guess that rule really is true: *Practice makes perfect.*

I was going to start practicing a lot more. Practicing everything . . . ballet, my acting, being a veterinarian. Missy was a total inspiration! If she could do it, why couldn't I?

I completely wanted a trophy like hers in my room. Not a baton-twirling trophy, of course.

But not a picture of me dressed like what I wanted to be someday (not a pirate, but an actress slash veterinarian), either.

Although doing stuff like going to Glitterati could be fun (if you did it with your actual friends) once in a while. If it didn't distract you from your *real* goals, and from practicing.

Missy took her victory coolly. She wasn't a sore winner.

"I should have won in the dance category, too," she said casually.

But you could tell she didn't mind coming in second in that event. So long as she had her trophy.

"You know," Courtney said to me later, "your friends at your new school are nice. You're really lucky."

This time, I didn't correct her.

"Thanks," I said, looking fondly at Erica, Sophie, and Caroline as they stood throwing popcorn at one another. "I know."

Unlike Missy, I *was* really lucky.

I was lucky I had escaped Walnut Knolls and come to a school with much nicer girls.

But more than that, I was lucky that my friends liked me, quirks — such as not liking tomatoes, loving rules, and liking acting, animals, and pretending things — and all.

These were the best kind of friends to have.

Allie Finkle's
RULES *for* GIRLS

- Do not touch anything in Missy's room.
- No talking in Missy's room unless Missy says you can talk.
- Leave Missy's room the minute Missy says so.
- Break the rules, and Missy will break *you*.
- Always agree with everything Missy says if you want her to stay in a good mood.
- It's important to try not to hurt someone's feelings if you can help it.
- Do not slam doors.
- Don't interrupt people.
- Never eat anything red.
- Breaking a promise to do something with one person, just because someone else asked you to do something way more exciting, is a rotten thing to do.
- If you are going to lie to other people about why you aren't going to do something with them that you said you were going to, you had better make it a really good lie.
- Being overly concerned about your health can be unhealthy.

- It's okay to lie if no one finds out you're lying, and the lie doesn't hurt anyone, and it isn't that big of a lie, and it's partially based on something true. Sort of.
- Nothing will get you in bigger trouble than lying.
- Liars don't get any of Harmony's home-baked cookies. Unless they cry hard enough.
- A present should come from the heart.
- Sometimes no matter how hard you try, you just can't win.
- *Thank you very much for having me* is what you say when someone invites you to a birthday party.
- Saying *yes, ma'am* and *no, sir* are other things you have to say to grown-ups when you're invited somewhere.
- Boy-crazy girls don't understand that not all boys are great.
- You can't do something to make the birthday girl unhappy on purpose on her birthday.
- Just because you're dressed like something doesn't mean you're magically going to transform into it when you're grown up.
- It's all good practice for later, when it really counts.

- It's important always to thank your hostess when you've had a nice time . . . and even when you haven't.
- Throwing food on the floor is bad manners.
- There *is* such a thing as a tesseract.
- Sometimes, the brave thing to do is go home.
- Always be true to your friends, just as you are to yourself.
- Part of preparing to have a future career as an actress slash veterinarian — besides reading every book you can find in your school library about animals — is that you have to be ready for every acting challenge that comes along.
- Saying the words "throw up" can make people who feel like throwing up actually do it.
- Practice makes perfect.